BUTCHERS

Todd Sullivan

Nightmare Press
Louisville, KY

Nightmare Press is the horror imprint of Frightening Floyds Publications

Cover Art by Holly Wholahan
Graphic Design by Rebecacovers

Thank you for reading! If you like the book, please leave a review on Amazon and Goodreads. Even if you don't like it, please still leave a review. Reviews help authors and publishers spread the word.

To keep up with more Nightmare Press news, join the Anubis Press Dynasty on Facebook.

To my parents, for their continued support.

-- Love, Todd

BUTCHERS

Todd Sullivan

CHAPTER 1

Tonight, Min Gun brought his butchering tools.

He clung to the surface of a rough brick wall five stories up. A bone saw attached to his belt by a thin chain swayed gently in the autumn breeze. He had sheathed his machete on his back beneath a rolled rubber body bag. He gazed into the dark room across from him. Cheol Yu, the target, hadn't left the building since he'd met Sey-Mi, a high school student wearing a plaid skirt and short-sleeved white shirt. Somewhere, behind the opaque windows of the apartment, Cheol Yu was with her, alone.

Min Gun's superior, Jun Young, clung to the wall beside him. A wood-handled axe dangled in a leather sling at his side, his machete strapped to his waist. Where Min Gun carried a body bag, Jun Young had a leather weapon case strapped to his back. The company had tasked the two with arresting the suspect. Min Gun hoped Cheol Yu resisted enough so that he would be forced to kill him, saving the man from months of torture.

That would be his noble deed of the day.

"It's been two hours," Jun Young said. "We have to assume he's not going to leave the building tonight."

These were the first words either of them had spoken since they assumed their positions after sunset, the shadows blanketing them from human eyes.

"We shouldn't wait any longer," Jun Young said. "I'll go around to his door. You enter through the window. If it comes to it, we've been authorized to reveal our abilities in front of the girl. She's to be protected at all costs."

Min Gun nodded, and concentrated on the living blood flowing through his dead body. He forced the latent spiritual residue to suffuse him, increasing his speed and strength for the upcoming fight with Cheol Yu.

His superior checked to see if any humans loitered nearby. The time approached ten o'clock, which was early for Seoul. Neighborhoods were often busy with people coming home from work, night classes, private tutoring, or the many restaurants and cafes throughout the city. Sinjeong was no different, and Jun Young had to wait for two women walking their dogs to pass. Then, he dropped five stories from the side of the building to the cracked concrete below.

Jun Young stepped out of the shadows and crossed the street. From their perch, they had watched the residents enter the passcode on the downstairs entrance. Jun Young now punched in the six digits on the keypad to unlock the outside door and enter the building.

Min Gun tightened his body and flung himself to the opposite wall. He landed soundlessly next to the target's window and placed his hand on the pane. It resisted his light push to slide it open, so he focused on the locked lever, reaching out to it with his mental energy. The metal knob turned to the unlock position. He then slid the window open and slipped noiselessly past the blinds into a dark room. He stood next to a neatly made bed and looked around. The door across the room was ajar, and through it he could see the target and the girl. They sat at a small table, the remains of a sweet potato pizza spread out between them. A variety show played quietly on a flat-screen television attached to the wall.

Min Gun watched Sey-Mi take a long drink. She then pushed a piece of shrimp onto the pizza, picked up the slice, and took a bite. Cheol Yu's hand rested on his cup as he stared at the television program. They seemed comfortable around each other to the point of intimacy, yet Min Gun knew that Sey-Mi would one day regret the rules Cheol Yu broke today. For a moment, he regarded her with deep pity.

Finally, Sey-Mi spoke. "It's gotten so late. I can stay here tonight. I'll tell my mom I'm studying at a girlfriend's."

An almost imperceptible change touched Cheol Yu's expression, and Min Gun tried to read the gaze he leveled upon the girl. To Sey-Mi, he wouldn't seem much older than her seventeen years. His thick, neatly cut hair covered the top of his ears and fell just above his eyes. He wore a loose striped shirt open to his chest, and a pair of casual black pants. Cheol Yu had stopped being human more than forty years ago, and even then, he had been nearing his thirties. Joining the organization had erased years from his appearance.

"Do you want to stay here? You've never spent the night before," he said gently and licked his lips.

Sey-Mi ran her hand through her black hair. She averted her eyes from his probing stare and looked down at the pizza. Min Gun inhaled to pick up the stinging sweet odor of the girl's nervousness and excitement crackling with a hot charge. Her heart rate picked up. Though no human would be able to hear it, to creatures like Min Gun and Cheol Yu, her heart was like a gong repeatedly struck. The reverberations rang throughout the apartment.

A knock at the door made Cheol Yu sit up. His facial expression registered mild surprise, but Min Gun saw the more subtle changes in the stiffening of his shoulders, narrowing of his eyes and hardening of his mouth.

Sey-Mi also looked up. "Someone else is coming over tonight?"

"Might be a visitor knocking at the wrong door." Cheol Yu stood. "You want a smoke? My cigarettes are just inside the bedroom."

Sey-Mi set her slice of pizza in the box, pushed back her chair, and stood. She went to the bedroom as Cheol Yu went to the front door. Min Gun leapt to the ceiling and hovered there as Sey-Mi walked under him to the bed. Cheol Yu didn't immediately open the door, and Min Gun sensed his struggle against the restrictions the company placed upon employees to limit their powers. Cheol Yu then reached out for the doorknob, but the door exploded open. Sey-Mi spun around in surprise at the sudden noise when Min Gun dropped from the ceiling behind her. He wrapped one arm around her waist, clasped his other hand around her mouth, and whispered, "Sleep."

The girl went limp in Min Gun's arms. He ducked to avoid Cheol Yu and Jun Young as they swept into the bedroom, a silent flurry of punches and kicks. They fought across the walls, the ceilings, their movements barely upsetting the apartment. Cheol Yu grabbed Jun Young by the throat and sank his nails into the other's flesh, drawing blood. Jun Young caught Cheol Yu's wrist with his left hand and punched upwards with his right, smashing his fist into Cheol Yu's elbow and breaking it into a sharp angle.

Cheol Yu grimaced. Not relinquishing his hold on Jun Young, he pounced forward through the open window, and the two figures disappeared into the night. Min Gun quickly laid Sey-Mi on the bed and sprang from the apartment after them.

Cheol Yu and Jun Young fought up the side of the building and tumbled onto the roof. Min Gun darted up the wall after them and hopped onto the rooftop. He saw Jun Young slide the parang machete from its sheath, raise it above his head, and bring it down with a powerful stroke into Cheol Yu's forearm. The blade only cut halfway into Cheol Yu's preternatural muscle and bone. Blood sprayed the gravel. With a growl, Cheol Yu pulled his leg back and kicked into Jun Young's chest, once, twice, a third time. Jun Young's ribs snapped beneath the force of Cheol Yu's heel.

Jun Young raised the parang machete to chop down again on Cheol Yu's gaping arm wound, but Cheol Yu yanked Jun Young to him before he could finish the strike and bit into his eye. A cry of pain escaped Jun Young's lips, and the surrounding buildings threw back a guttural echo. Cheol Yu pulled back and spat the pulpy eyeball out of his mouth, tendrils of blood dangling from his lips. Jun Young swung the blade again and cleaved deeply into the muscle of Cheol Yu's shoulder.

Min Gun leapt onto both men. Crawling over both, he straightened his hand and speared his fingers into Cheol Yu's arm. He grabbed the fleshy bone beneath the bicep and yanked upwards. A long howl billowed forth from Cheol Yu, and he flung himself to the rooftop, taking Jun Young and Min Gun with him. He rolled, bucking and twisting until Min Gun lost his purchase on top of him and slid across the bloody gravel. Jun Young still held tight, however. Raising the parang machete, he swung down at Cheol Yu's head. Cheol Yu dodged to avoid a direct blow to his skull, and the blade sliced through his ear, severing it from the side of his head.

Cheol Yu pounced into the air, a shower of blood raining from his injuries. He crashed back into Jun Young with his knee and cratered the rest of his rib cage. Min Gun raced forward, wrapped his fingers in Cheol Yu's neatly cut black hair, and yanked his head back. He snapped the bone saw from its chain and swung it down into Cheol Yu's neck. The jagged edge bit deeply into his flesh, and Min Gun started sawing through ligaments and nerves to the vertebrae with all of the enhanced speed of their kind.

"Don't kill him!" Jun Young shouted. "We're only authorized to arrest him."

Cheol Yu pressed his knee harder into Jun Young's torso, and his broken ribs ripped through his flesh. Cheol Yu dug his nails into Jun Young's chest cavity, tearing away at the sternum to expose his heart. Min Gun sawed even faster as he saw Cheol Yu's fingers wrap around the beating organ.

"Damn, damn, damn!" The words came from Min Gun in a wild torrent as Jun Young convulsed beneath Cheol Yu. Still, Jun Young had not released Cheol Yu, and despite his death throes, he feebly hacked away at Cheol Yu with the machete, to no avail.

"Damn!" Min Gun had only sawed halfway through Cheol Yu's cervical when Cheol Yu tore Jun Young's heart out of his body. He immediately tossed himself over Min Gun, who tightened his grip on the other's hair as Cheol Yu rolled over his shoulder. Cheol Yu snapped his head away, his hair ripping away from his scalp. His gaze settled shortly on Min Gun, his head tilted at an odd angle on his slashed throat. A grim smile on his face, he flung Jun Young's heart at Min Gun and spun away. Darting across the rooftop, he leapt to the next building, then the next.

Min Gun knew he should follow, but below him, he heard human voices disturbed by the screams. Quickly, he slid the body bag off his back and unfolded it. He retrieved the heart and stuffed it alongside Jun Young's body into the bag and hoisted the corpse onto his back. Already, he was in grave trouble for not capturing the suspect. He could not also allow the humans to find a retired *Gwanlyo* employee. With the heavy weight on his shoulders, Min Gun darted across the rooftop, down the wall and back through the apartment window where Sey-Mi slept. He took his phone from his pocket and punched in an emergency number to the *Gwanlyo*. Someone immediately picked up.

"A-Tour Travel Agency," a female voice on the other end said.

Keeping panic from his voice, Min Gun said, "My case number is 6288974. I need the aid of one who resolves."

"Drop a pin to your location. What's the current situation?"

A botched, failed mess, Min Gun thought. "A member of the Natural Police is dead. I have his body secured. I also have a female, sleeping. Human."

"Will she need to come with you?"

Min Gun paused. Sey-Mi wasn't scheduled for hire soon. But Cheol Yu had upset the carefully planned machinations of the company's managers. Now he simply wasn't sure what he should do with her.

"The target has fled," Min Gun said. "I don't think he'll be coming back to his apartment. The human may be able to remain here."

"Do you want to risk greater penalties, considering your actions tonight must have been flawed to the point of sheer incompetence?"

The words bore into him like nails, making him flinch. Min Gun closed his eyes to steady a trembling world. "We should move her somewhere else," he admitted, and turned as a light knock sounded at the door.

"That should be the *one who resolves*," said the voice on the other end. "The current details of your mission have been logged. That will be all."

The line went dead and Min Gun turned to the door to meet his fate.

CHAPTER 2

Cheol Yu slid open the window of his second apartment, located on the fifteenth floor of another building, and climbed in. Relief flooded over him. He had slept the day away in the cranny of Hanggang Bridge above Han River. He had feared the sun would touch him and burn him away, or a human would find him and alert others. In the weakened condition the Natural Police had left him, he had not wanted to travel far and risk being seen.

He was surprised when he awoke undisturbed the next evening, and immediately made his way to this apartment. Waiting for him was the only *Gwanlyo* employee that he could call for help.

Hyeri.

She stared at him in the dimly lit room, her gaze focused on his partially severed neck. Dried blood from his wound covered his tattered clothing. In this condition, he hadn't risked feeding. Any human who saw him like this would instantly struggle and scream, and would do all they could to escape the monster he appeared to be. He could only imagine how he looked to Hyeri, beat up the way he was. She would console him, though, offering what insight she could upon the situation he found himself in now.

"Hyeri…" he began, but before he could say more, Hyeri's mouth split open.

And she laughed.

The sound echoed in the silent room, her eyes brilliant with amusement. She pointed at the odd angle at which his head lay on his tattered throat, and then imitated him by craning her neck in the same way. She shook with laughter, blood forming at the corners of her eyes and leaking down her cheeks.

Cheol Yu closed the window behind him and lowered the blinds. "It's not funny." He tried to speak in a dignified manner, but this just made it worse. Hyeri doubled over and clutched her stomach, choking on the peals ringing from her mouth.

"Does it hurt?" she gasped out.

"What do you think?"

That brought her to her knees. Cheol Yu stared down at Hyeri, then sidestepped her and went into the bathroom. Hyeri crawled after him, her blood tears dripping on the floor. Cheol Yu stripped off his torn clothes while Hyeri regained her feet on shaky legs. She reached out and touched the gaping wound in his throat.

Cheol Yu flinched.

"I have to get my phone and take a picture!" Before he could protest, she rushed into the other room. Cheol Yu looked after her, sighed, and turned on the faucet. He grabbed the showerhead over the sink and washed the dried blood from his body. Every slight movement was a fresh spike of pain. When Hyeri returned, she pressed down on the home button of her phone to take a burst of photos.

"I wonder how sexy your little friend will think you are now." Hyeri held up the screen and scrolled through the images she'd just captured. Cheol Yu tried to snatch the phone from her, but she was quicker, and held the photos over him, gloating.

Cheol Yu shut off the shower and dried off with one hand while he balanced his head with the other.

"You know how long that's going to take to heal? You'll be stuck in the shadows when you're out in the mortal world. No way you can let a human see you looking like that."

"This would heal faster," he said, "if you let me have some of your blood."

"And ruin the fun?" Hyeri took another photo burst. "No way! I told you you were taking too long to feed from that girl. Of course the Natural Police were going to catch on eventually."

Hyeri was right. But he hadn't wanted to rush the feed, and he enjoyed talking to Sey-Mi, his great-grandniece. Cheol Yu had been born on the island of Jeju at the southern tip of Korea, and most of his family still lived there. It had been five decades since he had met any of his kin, and he missed them terribly. When he had been assigned to observe Sey-Mi, he recognized the resemblance to his people immediately. Doing some research, he discovered Sey-Mi was his sister's great-granddaughter.

Cheol Yu had wanted more than to just drink blood from her. He wanted Sey-Mi's love, and that took time to nourish.

"Fine, then." Cheol Yu pushed past Hyeri, who was still filming him, and went into the bedroom to dress. He had not logged this apartment in the neighborhood of Hyehwa with the *Gwanlyo*. If it had been closer to the study café where he met Sey-Mi, he would have brought her here instead. Asking a high school student to follow him halfway across the city late at night didn't seem like a good idea, so he had risked bringing her to his *Gwanlyo* sanctioned apartment instead.

That had been a mistake.

Cheol Yu took out the sewing needles that a previous tenant had left behind. He had never thought he would use them, but now he was glad he hadn't thrown them into the trash when he moved in. He went to his closet and ripped a silk shirt into thin threads. Getting a chair, he sat down in front of the mirror and slowly began to stitch his torn flesh together.

"Don't stare at me if you aren't going to help," he growled to a giggling Hyeri. After several moments, she put down her phone and took hold of the needle.

"I'll make a deal with you," Hyeri said. "I'll give you some of my blood so that you can heal faster, if you do something for me."

He already knew what her request would be. "No," he told her.

Hyeri pouted. "Why?"

"Because unlike you, I don't hate humans."

Hyeri didn't respond at first. Cheol Yu glanced at her in the mirror and saw that she'd become thoughtful.

"I don't hate humans," Hyeri said. "I just like to play with them, that's all. And the *Gwanlyo* keeps me from really having fun with mortals." She continued stitching his neck together. "I want to enjoy myself tonight, and I want you to be there with me."

The *Gwanlyo* had hired Hyeri when she was a teenager. Her position was to observe. She had a young face, and could easily pass for a middle or high school student. She interacted with teens most of the time, hanging around PC Bangs and amusement parks. Most days, like now, she wore a school uniform: a white blouse and tight dark skirt.

She'd been admonished by the *Gwanlyo* for breaking the rules in the past, and had been tortured many times in her ten years of service within the company. The last time the Natural Police had arrested her, those who dispensed justice had cut her open from her neck to her privates with a dull blade. They had pinned her flesh to the floor with rusty nails so that her body could not close and heal. Imprisoning her in a damp basement, they filled the room with starving rats that devoured her eyes and tore at her regenerating organs. She awoke at dusk screaming, and didn't stop until dawn the next day. She endured this treatment for months. By the end of her sentence, flies filled the room and maggots wriggled from her flesh like a coat of fur.

Hyeri finished the stitching. She had done a good job, but the black silk threaded through his neck stood out starkly against his pale skin. With her blood, a wound like this would take weeks, instead of months, to fully heal.

"Do this with me," Hyeri said to Cheol Yu, "and you can drink from me."

Cheol Yu sighed. "When?"

"Tonight." Hyeri's eyes were shining. "Before you change your mind."

Indulging Hyeri's disposition to hurt humans probably wasn't a good idea. He pushed her away, stood, and dressed in jeans, long sleeved shirt, and a light jacket with a high collar. He looked in the mirror again, but the collar didn't hide the jagged line of the stitching. He was extremely pale from the loss of blood, and couldn't remember the last time he looked quite so dead.

"You're not the pretty boy right now," she teased him. "Not until you get some of this." She held out her arms and clenched her hands into fists so that the veins stood out starkly beneath her flesh. Hunger laced through Cheol Yu. His incisors tingled, and he struggled against the urge to grab Hyeri and take her by force. He was five times her age and could overpower her if he wanted. The desire to do so grew, his body tightening with pleasure at the thought of assaulting her. He met her eyes and saw the wicked curve of her lips as if she knew his inner turmoil. She stepped closer to him and placed her fingers on his chest. His body convulsed at her touch, but he managed to restrain himself. The tension threatened to rip him apart, and in a strained voice, he said, "Let's go."

BUTCHERS

CHAPTER 3

Cheol Yu tore off the jacket and shirt and pulled on a hoodie. He grabbed a pack of cigarettes, went to the door, and imagined weights around his limbs and sand running through his veins. When he stepped into the hallway of the building, he walked at human speeds. Hyeri slowed down also to appear mortal. Reaching the elevator, Hyeri pressed the down button, and they stepped inside when the doors opened.

One floor down, the elevator doors slid open for a mother and her teen son. The teenager's eyes swept Hyeri's figure, once, twice, a third time. She favored him with a suggestive curve of her red lips. His mom frowned at her before she nudged her son to turn away.

Hyeri stood a head shorter than Cheol Yu. She had long black hair and a face that drew the attention of males. The boy kept glancing at her despite his mom's disapproval, his acne-covered cheeks blushing. The elevator door opened again several stories down and a young couple arguing about where to go for dinner got on. The mother and son took a step back to give them room, and the teen positioned himself close to Hyeri, his body tilted towards her. Hyeri took a small step to him until their feet touched. The boy quickly glanced at his mother, who didn't seem to notice.

Cheol Yu shook his head. He genuinely didn't hate humans. If anything, he was apathetic to their existence. As a *Gwanlyo* employee, he needed humans in order to continue living. The fact that he had once been mortal seemed distant, as it quickly did to all employees. The company made sure of that during the perverse training they all endured when first hired. New hires were stripped of their humanity even though they would be required to mimic human behavior when out in the real world. Failure to do so would draw the attention of Natural Police and result in severe penalties once arrested.

When the elevator doors opened at the lobby, they all got off and walked outside into an autumn evening covered by heavy clouds. Tall apartment buildings sprouted out of the gray concrete. Coffee houses, restaurants, and stores lined the streets. Kids chased each other along the sidewalks and played in the green parks dotting every block, their shrieks filling the dying day.

Hyeri set the pace, leading the way at a leisurely stroll. It took only a moment for Cheol Yu to notice they were following the mother and son. When the two entered a King's Mart, one of the many neighborhood grocery stores, Hyeri led Cheol Yu to a bench in an adjacent green space. They sat and lit cigarettes, the gray smoke curling before their faces.

“You know,” Cheol Yu said, “you’re going to end up back in the torture rooms if you keep this up.”

Hyeri’s face remained blank. A heavy, wet wind rustled the leaves above them. Cheol Yu imagined Natural Police concealed in the shadows of the branches, watching them, taking notice of every word.

"I'm tired of playing by their rules, going where they tell us to go, doing what they tell us to do." Hyeri took a deep inhale of her cigarette. "We’re supposed to live under their regulations till the end of time? Are you kidding me? If I could, I'd kill them all. Every last *Gwanlyo* superior. I’d set us all free to play in any way we want in the human world. No rules, no more inhibitions. Can you imagine it? Being free from the organization to do exactly what we like, when we like, how we like, without fear of punishment?”

They sat shoulder to shoulder. Cheol Yu felt resentment rolling through her body, and it infected him. He gritted his teeth. The *Gwanlyo* neutered employees to keep their powers under control. None of them knew what their unchecked abilities would really be like, or what they could do in the mortal world if they became who they were capable of being.

Though Cheol Yu would never admit this to Hyeri, he thought it was a good idea that her powers were restricted. When she had been mortal, her uncle had birthed something inside of her that was twisted and ugly. He had been a steel worker in a factory on the outskirts of Seoul. He raised her for a while after her mother disappeared into a brothel in Japan. Her father had died years earlier, drowning blind drunk in the Hyeongsan River after work one late night.

Now, she sat here in the park contemplating casual murder. Cheol Yu wondered if she knew that the impulse came from a place deep inside where her uncle still held sway over her all these years later. He wondered if she realized she was still that child in the corner who hated a world that did nothing to help her as she screamed.

The mother and son came out of the King's Mart, each carrying a full grocery bag. Cheol Yu stood alongside Hyeri, and they followed them back to the apartment building. They let the two of them enter the front door, then went around to the back of the building. Keeping to the shadows, they quickly scaled the rough wall, slid the stairwell window open on the fourteenth floor, and slinked in. The time neared ten o'clock, and many families were settling in for the evening. Each floor had five apartments, and voices drifted from behind closed doors as Cheol Yu and Hyeri walked down the hall to stand in front of the elevator.

They watched the numbers light up in the display panel. When the doors silently slid open, Cheol Yu stepped into the path of the mother as she and her son tried to step out. "Sorry," he apologized with a smile, his gazed locked on hers swallowing her attention as the teen stepped off the elevator next to Hyeri.

Normally, seduction would be simple. With the way he looked now, however, Cheol Yu was forced to exert his will over the mother's. She stared at him, blushing as they bumped into each other. She looked to be in her early 40s, and had a pretty face and long brown hair falling neatly to her shoulders. Slim, she wore a red skirt, a short-sleeved blouse, and heels. When she moved to the right to pass him, Cheol Yu moved to his right to let her pass, and they bumped into each other again. He placed his hand on her hip.

"We keep getting tangled," he teased, and she laughed. She moved to his left, and he moved to her left to let her pass as her waist touched his. His hand swept down her hip to her butt, and her blush reddened, her eyes never leaving his. He could smell it, her blood heating, and a quick penetration of her thoughts revealed a husband back home who, at this moment, she'd let wait forever. Cheol Yu pulled her close, her nipples to his chest, his thigh between her legs.

"Let me," he said, and in a swift moment that left her disoriented, he thrust her out of the elevator so that she stumbled. A low gasp of regret slipped from her parted lips, and Cheol Yu gave her a slight bow as the elevator doors closed. He exited on the next floor, went up the stairwell, and stepped through the shed outside onto the roof of the building. The air was wet with mist, an empty clotheslines stretched from one end of the roof to the other. The city spread out around him, tall buildings with lights shining from their windows. Voices floated up from the street like ghosts, while the occasional horn blast from an impatient driver tore through the night. In the distance, Han River cut blackly through Seoul.

Cheol Yu approached Hyeri and the teen standing near the edge of the building. Their tongues wrestled, the teen's hand under Hyeri's skirt. Two small wounds already marked the boy's throat. He opened Hyeri's shirt to expose her breast and bent to suckle it. Hyeri caught Cheol Yu's gaze and grinned, her incisors stained red.

Before she did it, Cheol Yu read her intention clearly. She took a small step, backing the teen closer to the edge, her eyes never leaving Cheol Yu. She took another step, and another, until they were off the side of the building. For the briefest moment they hovered in the air, Hyeri's hair floating around her head in the breeze, her eyes shining bright red as laughter erupted from between her lips. In the next instant, she was back on the ledge. The teen dropped, his hands grasping at air. His eyes never left Hyeri's as he fell, and Cheol Yu wondered if the teen even knew he rushed to his death when he slammed into unyielding concrete fifteen floors below.

Hyeri leapt on Cheol Yu, her legs wrapped around his waist. She whispered, "Thank you", repeatedly between feverish kissing. Their clothes disappeared from their bodies. Cheol Yu penetrated her, and they rode the waves of their emotion. Sirens below rent the night, and when the footsteps of humans echoed in the stairwell leading to the roof, Cheol Yu and Hyeri leapt to the next building.

Finally, they committed the last and most intimate penetration, their incisors extending to bite into each others' necks to drink. Cheol Yu forgot himself as he became Hyeri in the last memory she had of her mother, who hovered over her daughter, the alcohol on her breath strong enough to sting Hyeri's nose. Her mother's image faded away to be replaced by another: the gray man, wrapped in smoke and shadows.

Later, they lay naked beneath a dark sky, their limbs intertwined. "I feel," Hyeri said, "alive."

Cheol Yu kissed her shoulder. "But you still want more?"

She nodded. "I do, but for you this time."

His eyes widened, surprised. "Me?"

"I saw your secrets," she said. "Your innermost desires that you've been afraid to indulge. But it doesn't matter anymore, does it? The Natural Police are hunting you, so what have you got to lose?"

She raised her wrist, sliced it opened, and pressed the wound to Cheol Yu's mouth. "They'll be hiring Sey-Mi soon. But we can take her from them. Everyone hates the job most in the beginning, so it'll be easy."

Cheol Yu sucked hungrily at Hyeri's wrist as he considered her words. Could he entice Sey-Mi to join him? He would only be getting her into trouble. The Natural Police would eventually catch them and torture them back into obedience. She had been safe from the company as a human, but if she had already become what they were, if she had already accepted the job, then she had agreed, of her own free will, to exist under their regulations. There'd be no escaping that pact.

Could he inflict such a fate upon her? Cheol Yu had worked so long and hard to develop her trust so she would love him. For all of his efforts, he hadn't even drunk from her to taste the blood ties that bound them. He had never had the pleasure of living in his past again, and with the family he had lost.

Cheol Yu met Hyeri's gaze. A wide grin stretched her lips. She had him, and she knew it.

CHAPTER 4

Within the pulsating darkness, Sey-Mi heard a single word: Awake.

The command split the shadows apart, and Sey-Mi sat up. She inhaled sharply, her heart leaping into her throat. She was in a strange room. No matter how hard she searched her thoughts, she couldn't remember how she'd arrived there.

That couldn't be a good sign.

She was on a bed. The thin cover had slid to her hips when she sat up, and she threw it aside. A light overhead illuminated white walls with dark smudges smeared along them. Besides the bed, the room was empty except for a man who crouched at the door across from her. His fingers rested on a tall, dusty bottle, and he stared at her.

She had never seen him before. He wore a tight, short-sleeved shirt that clung to his muscular chest and arms. His sleepy eyes maintained an intensity that bore into her. She flushed as she tried to think of something to say to break the silence. Had he been watching her as she slept? Had he touched her, or done more to her, while she was submerged beneath the swirling darkness of her dreams?

Her temperature rose, and a light sweat broke out on her skin. Sey-Mi made a quick check of her clothes. She was still dressed in her school uniform. Her skirt, underwear, and shirt remained properly arranged. She couldn't even guess the time, the room having no windows.

If this guy decided to do something to her now that she was awake, would anyone hear her scream?

Her world spun sharply at the thought. Sey-Mi shut her eyes tight as she tried to calm down. She had to find a way past this guy and out of this room; but how? She opened her eyes and took his appearance in again, the studs in his ears, the dragon tattoo whorling down his arm, his raven black hair, shaved on the sides and swept up to form a wave on top. Why did he gaze at her so intently, as if trying to bore his way into her thoughts?

Sey-Mi noticed that he had not moved since she'd awoken – not a muscle, not a centimeter, his eyes unblinking. He looked as if he wasn't alive. She began to count the seconds in her head. When a couple of minutes had passed in which he still did not move, Sey-Mi cleared her throat and asked, "Are you real?"

He didn't respond, yet she sensed his shift at her question.

"Where am I?"

"You're in a building in Banghwa." His voice startled her. He spoke softly, yet his tone conveyed promises of pleasure and threats of torment. A thrill went through Sey-Mi as images of what this lone male could do to her in this isolated bedroom flashed in her mind. She exhaled long and low. She sensed incredible danger in him, and it drew her and terrified her at the same time. She could almost feel his hands on her body—probing, caressing, and tearing away at her simultaneously.

"Why am I here?"

"Because I have been given the task of posing a question to you," he replied. "Do you want a job?"

Sey-Mi laughed. Of everything she had imagined him saying, that wasn't it. A job? Could he be serious? The expression on his face did not change, and she laughed again at his seriousness, the peals spilling from her lips to ring in the windowless room.

"My parents," she said between gasps, "they would never allow me to work."

"Your parents aren't here."

In fact, beyond the room, Sey-Mi heard nothing. There were no sounds of footsteps on the floor, no drone of traffic, no voices. She felt disconnected from the rest of life, as though the two of them were all that existed. Still, her parents must be out there somewhere. They would never let her get a job. They only wanted her to study for end-of-winter exams so that she could get into one of the top universities in Seoul.

"I'm sorry," she said. "I can't get a job. It just isn't possible."

"You should accept my offer." He did not raise his voice, but the threat in his tone became palpable, growing to dwarf her on the bed. He still didn't move towards her, yet Sey-Mi leaned back from him, her back bumping into the wall behind her. It took her several moments to gather the courage to speak again.

"What happens if I refuse?"

"If you refuse," he said, "I'll tear your throat out and drain you of blood. I'll bring in a bone saw after you're dead. I'll dismember you and feed your bloodless corpse to prisoners of the *Gwanlyo*. They will curse their fate, but they'll be forced to devour every part of you until there is nothing left. No bone or teeth or hair left of your existence. You will vanish from the earth into their stomachs, and you will never be heard from again."

The words washed over her like a storm surge, sucked her deep into the horror like an undertow at the casual way the stranger described the violence he would render. It was no idle threat. He meant everything he said, of that there was no doubt.

Her heart ratcheted up again to a wild beat. Tears filled her eyes and slipped down her cheeks. "Why?" The question came out alongside a sob. "I didn't do anything to you!"

"This is nothing personal. I do not care if you refuse my offer of employment. But out there," he inclined his head to the door, "management makes the rules. I am simply the messenger. To be honest, hiring isn't my job, so I'm not very good at it. We don't normally conduct business in this manner, but your case is special."

She was sobbing now and could barely focus on him through her tears. This had to be a dream. Reality didn't work this way. Yet the bed beneath her, the wall at her back, her clothes…everything felt so real. No matter how much she wished it to be otherwise, this was not a nightmare.

"I'm not special." Her voice shook, and she found producing words difficult. She wanted to get out of the room back to her parents. "I didn't do anything to deserve this. I'm a good girl."

"Are you?" There was another shift in his mood that didn't play out on his face, yet she sensed it all the same. Suddenly, she realized that though this was the first time she had laid eyes on him, this wasn't the first time he had seen her.

"You didn't bring this current predicament upon yourself," he said. "That was done by another. Cheol Yu."

Cheol Yu? But that didn't make sense. She'd never been treated better by anyone her entire life. Cheol Yu had treated Sey-Mi as if she were the most important thing in the world. Coming from someone as handsome as him, that treatment had made her feel incredibly special.

Cheol Yu could have been a famous actor who had walked from a movie straight into her life. He had recently graduated from high school, and was a freshman at Sogang University. She'd first met him at a study café that she and her friends visited in Omokgyo. They saw him one day sitting by the window overlooking the city streets, a tablet and books spread out on the table before him. They had sat behind him, their eyes often lifting up from their books to stare at him. He drank many cups of coffee while he was there, and the café worker smiled brightly and took longer with him than she needed. Sey-Mi and her friends were jealous, wishing it was them who had the chance to speak with him.

Every day that they went to the study cafe, he was there at his usual table, studying. The café was on the fourth floor, and one day, Sey-Mi went to the bathroom on the first floor next to a Baskin Robbins. The male/female bathrooms were across from each other down a long, narrow hall. As she was coming out, he was going in. They had to pass close to each other. Sey-Mi couldn't believe it. She had been staring at him alongside her friends for the entire month, and now he was walking towards her. She cast her eyes down to the tiled floor, her face flushing with nervousness. She didn't know how it happened, she was paying very close attention to her body, but she still managed to accidentally bump into him. She quickly turned to apologize. Their gazes met. In those seconds, time became lost. They stood so close that she could feel his gentle breath on her face.

"You come to study here often?" he asked in a soft voice.

"It's for my final exams," she explained. "I need to get into a top school."

He nodded. "I can help you." He lifted a hand up, and between his fingers was a business card. "I work part-time at a hagwon. I also do some private tutoring on the side. I'm free to meet you most days."

He handed her his card. Their hands touched, and a thrill raced through her. Sey-Mi's knees went weak, and she feared they would buckle. She forced herself to remain steady on her feet so that she wouldn't make a fool of herself. She had never experienced a moment so intense in her life until now, in this windowless room, with the stranger threatening to kill her if she didn't take his job offer.

"What did Cheol Yu do? Please, tell me," she pleaded with the stranger. "He was always so kind."

Sey-Mi's feelings had developed quickly for Cheol Yu as he tutored her on math and science, English and history. He had suggested they go to another café that was more intimate. It was a tiny place tucked away in an alley in Mokdong. They had to sit close, and their legs often brushed together as he helped her with exam preparation. Concentrating proved difficult. She wanted to impress him so he wouldn't think she was wasting his time, but every time he turned his eyes upon her, her pulse raced and the information she tried to retain would slip through her grasp. Cheol Yu remained patient, which she always appreciated.

One late evening, when her stomach grumbled loudly and her face turned red at the fear that he heard, Cheol Yu invited her to his nearby apartment for takeout.

"I don't cook," he apologized with a sheepish grin.

She put her hand on his arm. "I don't care," she said. They gazed into each others' eyes, not moving for several moments, before he led her to his apartment. He ordered pizza, and gave her a beer.

"Just one," he said. She nodded. She had drunk alcohol before, but always at home or with her girlfriends. She had never had a beer with a guy who wasn't family. For that matter, she had never been in a guy's apartment like this, just the two of them, alone. She could see her father, angry beyond words that she was there. She could hear her mother, ashamed that her daughter would decide to be in this room with this university guy. Sey-Mi was doing something forbidden, something that high school girls at the top of their class didn't do. The thoughts of what Cheol Yu may do to her made her heart pound with excitement.

Cheol Yu had a big apartment with a separate bedroom, bathroom, living room, kitchen, and even a balcony. Tall speakers stood against the wall. Leaning against them was a black guitar case.

"Can you play?" she asked. He immediately took out the electric guitar and played a fast k-pop tune while they waited for the pizza to arrive. They smoked on the balcony, standing shoulder to shoulder, yet he hadn't kissed her that night, or the subsequent nights. As the evenings passed, Sey-Mi began to think that he only saw her as a student he was tutoring. But how, with the way he gazed at her, his eyes hungrily probing her? He had to see her as something more. He had to desire her for something else.

Finally, she got the courage to ask him if she could spend the night. To her relief, he had seemed on the verge of agreeing. There had been a knock at the door, and she had gone into the bedroom to get Cheol Yu's cigarettes.

That was yesterday, and now she sat on the bed in this silent room with a strange man asking her an even stranger question.

Sey-Mi craved a cigarette. Her hands shook, and all she wanted was to calm down and focus on the situation to figure a way out of it. She wiped the tears from her face with the backs of her hands, and smeared her makeup across her cheeks. Inhaling deeply, she fought to steady her voice, and asked, "What's the…" She paused. "Job?"

"You will work for the *Gwanlyo*," the man said. "I don't know in which function yet, but two new positions opened up recently. You will be given one or the other."

"Do you work for them?" Sey-Mi inhaled again. "The *Gwanlyo*?"

"I do."

She exhaled long and low as she rolled the next question around in her head. She didn't know if she wanted to hear its answer, but she knew she had to ask. She needed to go into this with as much information as possible.

"What do you do?"

"What they tell me to," he said simply. "Officially, I am a Natural Police."

Sey-Mi's eyes widened. "You're a cop?"

He hesitated "Yes. For the organization."

"You arrest people?"

The stranger nodded.

"These people," Sey-Mi began, "did they break the law? Did they do something bad?"

He hesitated again. An odd look crossed the stranger's face as if he wasn't sure how to answer the question. A second realization struck Sey-Mi. She didn't look away from him, but she felt sure that someone was watching them. They were under observation, and this stranger had to be careful what he said. But why? The threat of death hung over her, but what would happen to him if he failed in recruiting her?

"The people I arrest broke *Gwanlyo's* law," he said, "so yes, they did something bad."

The wording didn't make sense to Sey-Mi. "I don't think I could arrest someone," she said. "I'm not strong or anything. I don't exercise, and I don't know how to fight. That can't be the position they would put me in."

"Perhaps," the guy said.

"So what steps do I have to take," Sey-Mi asked, "if I decide to join your organization?"

"First, you would have to state clearly, without any question of your intent, that you are accepting a position in the *Gwanlyo*."

"And then what happens?"

"There's some paperwork you have to fill out. Your housing will be decided upon. After that, your training begins."

"My housing?" Panic wound its way through Sey-Mi. "What do you mean? Won't I be living at home?"

With his unblinking eyes, the stranger's gaze burrowed into Sey-Mi. "You will never go to your old home again." He spoke the words without emotion. "You will never see your mother or father, your younger brother, your grandparents, your cousins, your friends. All of these are now forbidden to you."

The words struck Sey-Mi like blows rained down by a vengeful god. She recoiled and choked on her breath. A sob was born within her and a low moan escaped her trembling lips. She bent over, the fresh tears pattering the bed covers. The moan became a pained cry that knifed her insides. The world spun faster. Sey-Mi closed her hands into tight fists hoping to control the contorting reality that had engulfed her. Finally, the wail slipped from her in relentless waves until her shrieks filled the room with her despair.

Time ceased to exist. Sey-Mi cried until tears no longer flowed. She screamed until her voice became hoarse. She hit her hands against her thighs, against her sides, hard blows to wake herself up from this nightmare. This could not be true, this could not be reality! She would not allow this to be true, she would not allow this to be anything more than a terrifying dream. Sey-Mi raked her legs with her nails, digging deep into her flesh and tearing bloody gashes across her skin. She did the same to her neck, ripping at her throat, then her cheeks. If she did enough damage, she would wake up and be in her bedroom again. If she hurt herself enough, this moment would end. Sunlight would stream through her window at a new dawn. Her mom would have breakfast prepared, her dad would have just come in from his morning walk, and her brother would be playing in the bathroom splashing water on the floor.

Yet no matter what injury she inflicted upon herself, the room and the strange man did not melt away. Everything she did only left her pained and exhausted. Eventually, the sobbing stopped. Hopelessness took its place, filling her until her limbs felt weighed down by a heavy depression.

"This can't be happening," she whispered. "This can't be reality."

"It is reality." The strange man had not moved during her tantrum. He had not stopped her from damaging herself, and showed no reaction to her current battered and torn appearance.

"You will never see your family again," he repeated. "But remember the alternative. If you refuse my offer, you will be killed, and then you will never see them again anyway. No matter what decision you make, your family is lost to you for all time."

Gradually, the hopelessness parted and was replaced with something else. Maybe he thought he could keep her from seeing her family again, but as long as this job was in Seoul, she would find a way. The city was big, and this company, the *Gwanlyo*, would not always be watching her. She would slip from their grasp when she could, she would escape them and return to her family.

One day.

She tightened her mouth, her teeth grinding against each other. I promise, she thought to her family, I will see you again!

Sey-Mi lifted her head and met the stranger's gaze without flinching. A fire spread through her. Purpose filled her, and the fire became a blaze. It didn't matter who came before her, it wouldn't matter who tried to stop her.

Sey-Mi slid out of the bed and stood up before the stranger. "I accept your offer." Her voice was clear as the flames burned brightly inside of her. "I will join the *Gwanlyo*."

One moment the stranger crouched by the door, the next his body was pressed against hers, his arms around her, his face a hair's breadth from her face. Despite the surreal nature of all that had happened, Sey-Mi still couldn't believe when she saw the fangs, then felt them pierce her neck. A brilliant pain wrapped in ecstasy shattered her sense of self. Her last thought before becoming lost in the tortured pleasure was, *No way...Surely I'm not being turned into a...*

CHAPTER 5

Sey-Mi awoke, and immediately discovered her hands and legs were bound. A metal bar ran from the chains around her wrists to the chains around her ankles, trapping her in a fetal position. She was naked, lying on a filthy cement floor. A gag, tied tight between her lips, cut sharply into the sides of her mouth making it impossible for her to scream for help.

Despite being in complete darkness, Sey-Mi could make out her surroundings in stark detail. A single door stood at one end of the room. She could make out no other means of escape. She heard the flutter of wings before she noticed the moths dancing along the cracks in the bricks of the walls. Craning her head back and forth, she could tell the stranger didn't crouch in the darkness with her. Unlike before, she was alone. Sey-Mi didn't know if that was better or worse. A man could assault her as she squirmed helplessly on the floor, but having no one present meant she could be left to starve. The idea of a slow, torturous death sent a fresh wave of panic through her.

Gradually, she began to ache. Sey-Mi tried to determine what part of her body radiated with pain, but the sensation seeded itself within her limbs deep into her bones. It flowered throughout her flesh as the moments ticked by, and she soon panted from fear. She struggled against her restraints, the chains cutting into her wrists and ankles. Sey-Mi moaned, long and low. She had to free herself, had to get out of this room. She couldn't die here like this when she'd promised herself she would see her family again. She would not fail; she would not allow the *Gwanlyo* to defeat her.

Sey-Mi chewed on her gag and worked her jaw in vain to get the thick cloth to slip from her mouth. She wiggled on the ground, and managed to roll from one side of the room to the other. She didn't understand how she did it, but she flung herself up and slammed into the hard ceiling, only to crash back down to the floor. Still, the ache persisted, tearing at her insides as if it had claws that would rip her apart if she couldn't find a way to tame it.

She froze at the sound of the metal door opening, and twisted around to see a man enter. There was nothing especially threatening about him, but Sey-Mi squirmed back anyway until she slammed against the far wall. Her heart thudding dully in her chest, she pleaded with the man not to hurt her, but the gag stuffed into her mouth made her words sound like muffled squeals.

The man stared at her. No sympathy lurked in his gaze. He simply stared at her, the features of his face chiseled and handsome. He reached into his pocket, and Sey-Mi recoiled in terror, her body shuddering so that the chains rattled.

He withdrew keys and a phone.

"It's an honor to welcome you to the *Gwanlyo*, Sey-Mi." He bowed to her. "My name is Dae Lo. I will be the one who instructs you on proper protocol as a company employee. Under my tutelage, you'll learn what it is to carry yourself with decorum in the world of humans."

Sey-Mi stopped trying to burrow into the wall pressed against her back. She stared in disbelief at the figure standing before her. Nothing Dae Lo or the other man had said made sense to her. What did he mean she was no longer human? She had arms and legs; she still breathed and had a beating heart.

"Is that all humans are?" He stepped towards her. "Body parts? A beating heart? The ability to inhale and exhale?"

He considered her for several moments. "What if I chopped off your legs and arms, but they grew back in time? What if your heart stopped pumping because there was no more blood to run through it, yet you did not die? What if you only breathed air when you were on the hunt? Would you still then be human?"

He stared at her as if she could truly answer him through the gag. But what could she say? His words made no sense, and talk of chopping off her legs and arms sounded ominous. She was human, and she wanted to make sure her captor considered her such. If he didn't, if he saw her as less, what might he do to her?

The man held up the phone. "I have something to show you."

He moved towards her. Sey-Mi pushed backwards but could not avoid him. In another moment, he would be upon her. The thought made her scream, which came out as a muffled cry. Dae Lo crouched, took the metal bar in his hand, and dragged her to him. Grabbing her by the back of the hair, he yanked her head back and held the phone above her. No emotion crossed his face as she struggled against him. He slammed her head into the ground, twice, stunning her. Sey-Mi grew still as she fought against the darkness creeping along the edges of her vision.

"Now watch." He pressed play on the phone.

Sey-Mi couldn't focus until her vision cleared. He held her hair tight, her neck strained at the angle he forced upon her. She was looking at a room on the phone, and a person on the floor. It was a female, and she was bound by chains with a metal bar running from her wrists to her ankles. She was naked and gagged. It dawned on Sey-Mi that she was looking at herself, but how could that be? The cameras were barely recording her movements as she moved from one side of the room to the other. At times, her image was nothing more than a blur. At one point, she bounced up several meters to hit the roof before falling back to the floor.

She wanted to ask questions, but couldn't. The video recording had to be doctored. Dae Lo played it again, and again. Each time her actions were equally amazing, and impossible to comprehend. This couldn't be her.

"But it is you." Dae Lo released her hair, and her shoulders slumped forward. "The cameras aren't malfunctioning. You possess the speed and strength of *Gwanlyo* employees. With these new abilities, you will serve the company for the rest of eternity. However, in the mortal world, you must imitate humans at all times. You must move slower, and you must be careful of the strength you use in your every motion. Revealing in any way that you are now an employee of the *Gwanlyo* will be met with punishment. The more severe the display, the more severe the penalty. Remember that the *Gwanlyo* are always watching."

Dae Lo stuck the key into the lock that held her chains. "You will begin your lessons today, and I will assess your capabilities and record them. The company must still figure out what position you'll assume in the organization."

The chains fell away. Sey-Mi pounced to her feet and lashed out at the side of Dae Lo's face. Her nails raked across his left eye and shredded his pupil. A sharp cry of surprise erupted from him, but before he could recover, she swung with her other hand, slamming her knuckles into the bloody gash of his eye.

Dae Lo fell back with an anguished roar. Sey-Mi raced to the door, but only made it several steps before hands closed around her hair and yanked her back. She felt clumps rip from her scalp. She cried out but quickly got away and tried for the door again. Dae Lo suddenly appeared to her right and kicked out at her legs. Sey-Mi leapt over his foot and jammed her thumb into his eye socket, piercing the jelly-like mass beyond. Dae Lo's screams resounded through the room. Sey-Mi cupped the side of his face with her other hand and tried to rip his skull apart. The door suddenly flew open and shadowed shapes flew into the room. Hands grabbed her and slammed her to the ground. Sey-Mi could barely keep up with their movements as they subdued her with a constant barrage of viscous strikes. She heard her bones cracking, felt her body going soft as they beat her with unimaginable force.

"Enough!"

The stranger from before appeared in the midst of the figures pummeling her and ordered them back. Sey-Mi could not move, she could barely think through the haze of pain. No part of her body felt right, as if she was now just a mass of flesh heaped on the cement floor.

Dae Lo appeared in her vision, the blood from his destroyed eye raining onto her forehead. His face was no longer emotionless. Anger marred his scarred features.

"That," he hissed, "was a mistake that you'll have an eternity to regret."

CHAPTER 6

Killing the teen had filled Hyeri with a pleasure that ballooned inside of her, stretching her until she thought she would pop. Enlisting Cheol Yu to distract the mother so that she could get the teen alone on top of the apartment building had made the moment even more special. The ties between her and Cheol Yu had deepened, while feeding from each other had created an unbreakable bond. Hyeri would do anything to help him achieve his goal. She would make sure Cheol Yu won Sey-Mi, and by drinking the girl's blood, he would be able to relive his past.

First, Hyeri needed to figure out the best way to get Sey-Mi from the *Gwanlyo*. They would be watching her closely because she was a new hire. As Hyeri wandered the cold city streets, rode subways and busses, or watched students in PC bangs, study cafes, and libraries, she pondered the possibilities. But an itch developed as the nights wore on. It distracted her from her job and her determination to aid Cheol Yu. She needed to do something to find relief from the itch, and she couldn't ignore the siren call for long.

Hyeri wanted to kill another human.

She had gone through this phase before. Her last killing spree had lasted months before the *Gwanlyo* figured out it was her. After arresting her, they had tortured her relentlessly. At the time, she didn't think she would ever forget the constant, ongoing punishment for her transgressions. More than a year had passed, though, and her memory of those weeks cut open and pinned down to the floor had grown distant.

The image of the teen plunging from the apartment building played over and over in her mind. The expression he wore as he fell, his desire for her etched into his face until the moment he slammed into the concrete and the force shattered his skull. Hyeri woke up evenings laughing aloud to herself at the absurdity of it. Reality was a joke not meant to be taken seriously. She remembered life before this realization, when she was a child and was always crying. Now she knew better. Now she just wanted to laugh in the face of the world's unending cruelty.

She needed another human to amuse herself with, to make herself smile through their pain.

One day, she noticed a man with a golden watch. Evening came early, the sky turning darker shades of blue not long after five o'clock. Hyeri had dressed in her usual schoolgirl uniform: a tight plaid skirt and a white blouse. She wore a padded white jacket because all of the students were wearing one this winter. She went out into the night to begin her surveillance of a future employee, a thirteen-year-old girl who went to a middle school in the Gongdoek neighborhood. At a bus stop adjacent to the school's front gates, she saw the man.

He wore casual dress pants, shirt, and jacket. He sat on one of the benches beneath the bus shelter and waited. Middle school girls trickled out of the school gates and slowly collected into a sizable crowd. They chatted about stressful classes, teachers who assigned too much homework, and worried about upcoming tests. The man with the golden watch would stand amidst them and casually brush against their bodies, his hand pausing a breath too long on a hip here, a butt there. Most girls didn't notice those brief moments of contact. Those who did would step aside, but he seemed to especially like those moments. He wouldn't give them room, insistently pressing against them. Hyeri saw the discomfort on their faces, and read in their tense postures how they didn't want to make a scene, how they didn't want to draw attention to themselves. He took advantage of their reluctance, harassing them until the girls finally escaped his ministrations onto the bus.

It was those middle school girls, the ones who tried unsuccessfully to avoid him when he pressed against them, that brought back memories of Hyeri's uncle. Back in elementary school, her mom would leave Hyeri in his care in the evenings. She worked nights at *noraebangs*, and would return home early in the morning reeking of the whiskey her clients had brought her. Her father had died years earlier, drowning in the river. By accident or by choice, no one knew.

Hyeri's uncle smoked incessantly, one cigarette lit the moment the previous one was snubbed out. She used to think of him as the gray man, wrapped in smoke and shadows. The gray man would drink beer and soju, then call her to sit on his lap. She wanted to refuse, but this was still when she took the world seriously. Children obeyed adults in the serious world, and she could do nothing as his fingers slipped past her underwear to rub furiously against her.

One day, her mother didn't come home, and neighbors said she had gone to work in karaokes in Japan. Hyeri's uncle was given the responsibility to take care of her, and after school every day she came home to a house empty of all except smoke and shadows. Days became weeks, weeks became months. She started to tell him no; he started to hit her, driving her into corners with first a belt, then his open palms. One night he finished off bottles of beer and soju and woke her as she slept. When she rejected him, his palms became fists, pounding her until she was barely conscious. In that state he stripped off her pajama bottoms, pushed inside of her, thrust for minutes, then collapsed, spent, on top of her battered body.

This happened again, and no one did anything no matter how loud she screamed. The time she woke up half-alive in the hospital was the day healthcare workers took her. By then, Hyeri had begun to see the world differently. A joke, twisted and cruel, and she realized that it was better to laugh than to cry, funnier to give than to receive.

Then, just before her eighteenth birthday, the *Gwanlyo* hired her, and Hyeri finally realized how amusing life really could be.

In the alley near the bus stop, Hyeri observed the man with the golden watch remove a pack of cigarettes from his jacket pocket and smoke while he waited for the next group of girls to crowd around him. Hyeri decided she really wanted him to make her laugh, and stepped out to the sidewalk. She went to where he sat on the bench, and giggled. The man turned to her. His eyes widened slightly, his gaze quickly sliding down her chest, to her hips, to her thighs and back up again to her face. She didn't say anything at his naked appraisal. She sat down beside him so that their arms touched, and inhaled to pick up the distinct aroma of arousal flooding his body.

She felt him become tense. Out of the corner of her eye, she saw his hands shake. He raised the one nearest her, lowered it, inched it closer to her thigh, then cleared his throat and clenched his fingers together. He needed encouragement, so Hyeri casually leaned further into him and giggled again.

"Would you be angry if I asked you for a favor?"

The man jumped at her question, his surprise distorting his face as his mouth dropped open. He gaped at her, a light sheen of perspiration touching his upper lip. Finally, he found his voice. "Are you talking to me?"

Hyeri giggled. "Of course," she replied with a bow. "I was supposed to meet my older sister out here, but she's going to be late with her studies." She leaned closer to him so that her chest pressed against his shoulder. The man swallowed, his breathing quickening to short little bursts.

"What were you two going to do?" he asked, his voice strained, his eyes darting around before settling again on her face.

"School is so stressful, and we like to," she pursed her lips and brought two fingers together imitating a smoking gesture.

"You're too young," the man exclaimed. Hyeri laughed.

"You just don't know how difficult our classes are this time of year!" Hyeri lowered her lashes. "It's a bad habit, I know, but what else can I do to relax my body?" She focused on him again. "Could you buy me a pack of cigarettes? None of the convenience stores will sell to someone my age."

"How old is that?" The question exploded out of him.

"Not old enough," she said with a laugh.

He silently regarded her. "What will you give me if I do this for you?"

She answered with a smile, her body still pressed against his shoulder.

"Ok," he said. "There's a good store a few blocks away. Will you walk there with me?'

She nodded. Together they left the bench as a new group of girls crossed the street from the school. He led Hyeri off the main avenue and took a series of side streets that wound their way through squat apartment buildings with faded yellow walls. There were no sidewalks, so they walked alongside cars. The man waved off each corner store they passed.

"Too many people around these kinds of places." He glanced at her with doubt in his eyes, and she knew he was skeptical that she would fall for his excuses.

"Usually me and my older sister hide out behind buildings for a quick smoke," she admitted. "Otherwise someone will yell that we're too young. They'll ask what store sold us the cigarettes and say they're going to snap pictures and put them on social media to shame us."

"Right, right," the man quickly said. "You don't want that, it'll get you in too much trouble. But where I'll take you, you can do what you want." He brushed against her, his hand tapping her butt.

Hyeri followed him to a street of automotive businesses. Mopeds and scooters leaned against each other in front of open garages. Men in dark pants and grease-stained long-sleeved shirts worked over cars. The smell of oil filled the air. They passed a mechanic welding a narrow piece of metal, his goggles reflecting the steady flame of the blowtorch in the twilight. White dogs tied down by thick ropes paced back and forth in front of repair shops, or peered down from the rooftops. Cats slinked in the shadows and darted between the wheels of cars.

Finally, the man with the golden watch stopped in front of an electronic shop with tinted windows. He opened the door and stared back, waiting.

"Is this it?" She stared into the darkened interior.

"This is it," he assured her. "It'll be best if you smoke in here. No one will see you. It's completely safe."

Hyeri giggled and stepped inside. The man entered right behind her, closing and locking the door, then flicking on the light. The store was narrow but long. Shelves lined the walls, and rows of cameras and used phones ran along them. Manga was stored on several shelves, and beneath them were plastic CD cases of movies and pornography. Vaping pipes stood on a glass display case beside Zippo lighters, butane flasks, and packs of cigarettes.

"Please make yourself comfortable."

The man caressed her cheek, and Hyeri smiled. She turned from him and went to the vaping pipes. When she reached out to touch one, the man's arm draped around her waist.

"Those are very expensive." He moved the pipe out of her reach and held a dented Zippo before her instead. "I'll let you have this for a cheap price. Have you seen one of these before?"

With his thumb, he flicked the Zippo lid open and ignited a tiny flame.

Hyeri laughed. "It's too small!"

"That's an easy fix. You see, you put more lighter fluid in it like this." He separated the Zippo into two parts, pried open the bottom, and squeezed butane fluid into it. "Add a lot in it and you'll get a really cool effect. Like this."

He flicked the flint wheel again and an impressive flame erupted from the lighter. Hyeri squealed with glee and clapped her hands as he took two cigarettes from a pack, lit one for her, and one for himself.

Hyeri looked at the row of Zippos and one caught her eye. The man with the gold watch smoked behind her, his hand sliding down to her butt, down to the hem of her skirt and under. Hyeri reached for a black Zippo with an engraving of a golden skeleton snapping his finger and producing a spark. When she touched it, the man quickly slid it away from her.

"Too expensive," he said.

Hyeri smiled. She reached for it again, and when he tried to move it again, she snaked her hand past him and snatched it up with a giggle. The man's eyes opened in surprised.

"Wow," he said, "you're fast."

Hyeri stuck the Zippo in the waistband of her skirt. "You still want it?" she taunted him.

The man's hands trembled. "You like it that much?" His voice was breathy, and he swallowed several times. "Maybe I can let you have it, but what will you do for me?"

Hyeri snatched up the butane fluid with one hand and darted out with her other to clench around the man's throat. His mouth gaped open as she applied pressure, choking him. Hyeri stuffed the flask into his mouth and squeezed.

"I'll do this for you." She spun and slammed him into the display case. The glass shattered and she pressed him into shards that tore through his clothes into his skin.

"And this." She tossed away the flask, grabbed a vaping pipe, and jammed it into his eye. She tightened her fingers around his throat so that he could only croak out garbled screams. “And this.” She twisted out the pipe, entrails of blood and fluid stretching and snapping to leak down his cheeks, and slammed it into his other eye. Then she let him drop to the floor, a writhing heap grasping at his face. Hyeri lifted her foot and then forced his head down to the floor. His screams were loud, so she pushed down on his skull and easily cracked it under her heel, silencing him.

She looked around the store. “I guess this all belongs to me now,” she said to herself with a laugh.

CHAPTER 7

Hyeri opened the door to her apartment in Hongdae and saw a member of the Natural Police sitting at her desk. He had gotten into her MacBook and now scrolled through different files in the Finder Folder. She closed the door behind her with a louder thump than necessary so that he would be aware of her presence. He continued to tap away at her keyboard for several moments before swiveling the chair around to regard her.

Hyeri wondered if he was there because of the man she murdered the other night, or if he was there investigating any connection she might have to Cheol Yu. She'd been meeting Cheol Yu daily for the past two weeks. As promised, she let him drink from her to heal his partially severed neck. This act diminished her strength, and forced her to feed from two and three humans a night. If she didn't, maintaining focus became difficult as extreme fatigue crept over her.

Tonight, she had been busy dismembering the corpse of the man with the golden watch. She had cut him into pieces, wrapped the limbs in plastic, and carried them in weighted travel bags to Han River where she dropped them. Then she'd cleaned the electronic store with bleach and chlorine. When an upset flask of butane leaked into the chlorine, a chemical fire with white poisonous gas ignited. Only her unnatural speed got it under control before the orange tongues could spread through the cleaning fluid and engulf the store.

Once the electronic store was spotless of blood and gore, she had gone to Cheol Yu's apartment so he could drink from her. She only had enough time afterwards to feed on a young man closing a bar near Hongdae for the night, leaving him half-dressed, slumped over and barely alive in one of the booths. Hunger still tore at her; the lack of blood pumping through her heart put her in a nasty mood. The last thing she wanted to deal with was a member of the Natural Police. Yet here one sat in her apartment staring at her with the full authority of the *Gwanlyo* behind him.

Hyeri kept her tone neutral and asked, "Do you need something?"

She lowered her gaze to just below his eyes and pushed thoughts of Cheol Yu into a mental safe, which she dropped into the deepest pools of her mind. She dredged up images of the middle school girl she had been tasked to observe over the past year.

"I wouldn't be here if I didn't require something. My name is Min Gun. I have a matter to discuss with you." He stood. "An employee has gone rogue. We've been interviewing those who worked with him in the past to see if he's attempted to make contact. We believe he's hiding somewhere in Seoul."

The safe bobbed in the recesses of Hyeri's thoughts. Min Gun's questions tugged at it, and she became convinced he was attempting to read her mind.

"Sounds like a real problem." She laced her words with sympathy. "What's his name?"

"Cheol Yu."

Hyeri tilted her head slightly and created the expression of one seriously trying to recall a detail from the distant past. "I remember him," she admitted. "He was one of my first mentors in the company. He taught me how to remain unseen as I observed the human I was assigned to. He was skilled at making himself invisible. I think it will be quite difficult for you to locate him."

"Difficult, yes, but not impossible." Min Gun approached her. "And of course, if we discover that any *Gwanlyo* employee is helping him, they will be punished alongside him. In fact, greater would be their torture since they are aiding and abetting a criminal instead of showing undying loyalty to the company."

The phrasing almost made Hyeri break character. "Who would be so foolish as to help a rogue employee and risk the wrath of the *Gwanlyo*? Not when employees are powerless against the brutality of their disciplinary measures."

Perhaps that had been a little much. She waited for his reply, seconds passing between them in silence. Min Gun raised his hand and gently cupped her chin. He lifted her face to his, their eyes locking onto each other.

"Hyeri," he said softly, "please be aware of your precarious status in the organization. The managers are usually extremely reluctant to retire employees. They prefer methods of rehabilitation so that the employee can become a productive member of the company again. But even management has limits to their patience. You've had numerous infractions in your ten years of service. The *Gwanlyo* has done all it could to help you see the wisdom of their ways. But there have been discussions about you. Serious, on-the-record conversations about future penalties should you break the rules again."

He released her chin. "My advice to you is to strictly abide by the regulations and suffer no further stains on account of your behavior." He held a card out to her. "If you hear from Cheol Yu, call me at this number."

"I understand," Hyeri said, her voice quivering. "I don't wish to cause any more trouble. I haven't heard from Cheol Yu in years, but if I do, I will immediately contact you."

She took the card with trembling fingers. Min Gun went to her door, opened it, and glanced back at her one last time. When the door closed behind him, a wide grin stretched Hyeri's face from ear to ear. She darted to the window, slid it open, and crawled out onto the rough brick wall. Dawn would arrive within the hour. Already, the edges of the velvet sky were brightening as the sun fought against the darkness.

Min Gun exited the building and quickly navigated the narrow streets snaking down the steep hill of her neighborhood. Hyeri leapt from rooftop to rooftop, following him to the subway station. She quickly surveyed the area for humans before dropping into the shadows and going down the long escalator after him. She had to give him ample distance so that he wouldn't notice her, and began breathing to track the scent on his clothes. One of the odors on him was very familiar to her. She had detected the same on Cheol Yu. It was that girl, Sey-Mi. Min Gun must have recently been in her company.

Min Gun got on the 2 Line. Hyeri waited at the edge of the subway and slowly pulled shadows around her to hide herself from the CCTV positioned throughout the station. Her hunger spiked at this use of her power, and a growl slipped past her lips. When the train left the station, she leapt onto the back and clung to a railing as the subway rushed into the tunnel. She crawled to the top and crept down the shaking cars until she was over the compartment that Min Gun had entered. He transferred several stops later at Yeongdeungpo-gu Office. She rolled off right before the train left the platform and followed him to the Purple Line.

More humans filled the station here. Since she was breathing to track Min Gun, she also picked up the scent of their blood. Her incisors tingled as desire washed over her. Visions of tearing into their throats to feed, ripping out their jugulars so that the blood would wash over her face in delicious spurts, flittered through her mind. She heard the sunrays buzzing in the air around her. Light filtered down the stairs leading from the city above. She followed Min Gun out of Banghwa station. Enough sunlight penetrated the air that her skin burned with irritation.

Hyeri gritted her teeth and pushed forward. Min Gun disappeared down a long alley that carved through a cluster of decrepit buildings away from the main street. Hyeri considered following him, but the pain from the coming dawn pressed down upon her in concurrent waves. She could go no farther without passing out in the street.

Min Gun would be feeling the same way, so his final destination had to be close. Hyeri noted the location and rushed back into the subway. With the last of her strength, she summoned the shadows to crowd close around her. She slipped onto the tracks and stumbled down into the tunnels. Scooping up scattering mice and draining them, she left a trail of emaciated corpses behind. Then she collapsed into an alcove and pressed herself against the wall. A moment later, her conscious ceased to exist, leaving only a cold, lifeless body behind.

CHAPTER 8

The door opened. Sey-Mi watched Min Gun enter the basement. She lay in a fetal position on the floor, still naked, her wrists and ankles still chained. Her captors hadn't freed her since that first time when she ripped out Dae Lo's left eye. In the dark room, closed off from the outside world, Sey-Mi knew neither when day became evening nor night became morning. She simply realized that there would be a moment in which she seemingly ceased to exist. The next moment, she would be aware again. She could only guess at how many hours had passed during the interlude.

Dae Lo had kept his word. He had hurt her in ways she *could* imagine, and in ways she had never thought possible. In her previous life, before this room, she had been a teenage girl about to graduate from high school and attend college. She had been innocent, only having kissed boys before. Her secret crush on Cheol Yu had developed into love. That's why she had asked him that evening if she could stay at his apartment. She didn't know what he would say, but she knew she had to speak up. Her first experience of true intimacy was supposed to be the most special moment of her life, and with Cheol Yu, it would have been.

Dae Lo, and the men who accompanied him, had smashed that hope, stealing whatever was left of her childhood and burying it beneath disgusting filth. Their brutality and perversion had shocked her senses. Her body had suffered relentless torment as they'd worked her over. Often, Sey-Mi had been sure that she would lose her mind, yet after the daily assaults, each lasting for hours, they would leave her broken and battered but with steely resolve to see her family again tethering her to sanity.

Min Gun would often be there, watching, a dusty bottle in his hand. After Dae Lo's punishing treatment, Min Gun would go to her, place the bottle to her lips, and let the contents spill into her mouth.

Blood.

It filled her in a way nothing else had. No matter what Dae Lo did to her, the perversities faded from her thoughts as the blood poured down her throat. Drinking was the purpose of her life now, the pleasure it wrought upon her battered body exquisite. She hungered for it from the moment her eyes opened after the interlude of nothingness. Throughout the ordeal Dae Lo and his companions put her through, her thoughts lingered on the moment when the bottle would be placed to her mouth. The blood made her feel connected to life. As the dark red liquid poured into her, Sey-Mi grasped what it meant to be truly complete.

Min Gun's arrival now was unexpected. Dae Lo always came first. Sey-Mi didn't know how to feel about this. She hated Dae Lo, and though Min Gun never touched her, she partially hated him, too. He had witnessed what they had done to her, and when she met his gaze, she felt violated anew. Yet he carried the bottle, and until she knew how to get blood on her own, she needed him. She couldn't help the rush of desire his appearance brought out in her.

Min Gun knelt down beside her, removed the key from his pocket and inserted it in the locks. The chains fell away, freeing her. Min Gun didn't move further, and Sey-Mi didn't shift her position. Even if she wanted to, she didn't have the strength to attack him. Her heart didn't even beat in her chest, something that shocked her when she first noticed it after her imprisonment. It wouldn't start beating again until she drank the blood, but Sey-Mi didn't reach out to the bottle. In fact, she didn't move at all, and the two of them remained motionless in the darkness.

"Tonight," Min Gun finally said, "you leave this room. Your first stage of training has been completed." He held up the bottle to her. "Congratulations."

The news struck Sey-Mi like blows, and she flinched. What was she supposed to make of this announcement? After everything they'd done to her, would they now allow her to leave this room and go out into the world beyond? Did they not realize the overwhelming hatred she harbored for them?

Min Gun uncorked the bottle and leaned it towards her. She inhaled the metallic tang of blood. That alone was enough to warm her, a buzz of longing echoing inside her head. She reached out, expecting Min Gun to yank the bottle from her just to be mean spirited. When her fingers touched the smooth surface, she couldn't stifle a sigh of relief. She met his eyes and expected to see scorn in his gaze. His face remained impassive. She couldn't glean thoughts from his blank expression, but beneath the surface, something existed. Could it be sympathy? He was attempting to hide it. For some reason, he didn't want her to see it. After dealing with Dae Lo, she could understand why showing empathy for her in front of these people could be a mistake.

Yet she detected something different about Min Gun that set him apart from the others - something unmistakably kind.

She raised the bottle to her lips. The blood spilled into her mouth, its effects enhancing her senses. The details of the room became even clearer so that the cracks stood out against the brick walls. The scents of the outside world clinging to Min Gun became sharper and easier to identify. Within the blood, faint memories persisted. She heard whispers of the blood's owner, an old woman trying to accomplish more despite the loss of her youth. Tears and sadness over connections lost through time plagued the woman and seeped from the blood into Sey-Mi.

Sey-Mi's heart began to beat again, faint yet definite. She continued to drink, upturning the bottle and emitting a growl as she consumed more than she had previously been allowed. Strength returned to her. When the very last drops had slid out of the bottleneck and onto her tongue, Sey-Mi lowered the bottle to discover a smile touched her lips.

Nothing revealed itself in Min Gun's eyes, but she knew he was satisfied with her reaction.

"Come." He turned to the door. "It's time you left this place."

Sey-Mi set the bottle on the floor and followed Min Gun to the door. Often, she had wondered what was beyond it. She hadn't been outside of the room since they'd incarcerated her here. She had picked up the heavy odor of the Kang River, the sugary smell of a nearby bakery, and the lingering scent of perfumes. The men who'd assaulted her had stood close to humans, on either a bus or subway, before they came to work on her. Sey-Mi was sure of this.

Min Gun unlocked the door and opened it. Down a short passage, a steep stairwell led up into the darkness. To the right was a room with a showerhead and drain. Hanging from a nail in the wall were clothes and underwear.

"Take a shower," Min Gun said. "When you're dressed, go up the stairs. I'll be waiting for you there."

Min Gun went up to another door at the top of the steps and disappeared behind it. For several moments, Sey-Mi stood there in the dark. Her mind swirled with questions. Was she ready for the outside world? After what they'd put her through, Sey-Mi no longer felt quite human. How would she behave around regular people? What would she say if someone spoke to her? Even without having been told, she knew she was forbidden to reveal to anyone what had happened to her. But would she be able to keep the terrible abuse a secret? And what would happen if she couldn't?

Finally, Sey-Mi stepped into the bathroom. The showerhead was on a notch above a sink. On a shelf next to the mirror was a bottle of liquid soap, shampoo and conditioner. When she began to shower, rivulets of grime washed from her body and swirled down the drain. They had kept her filthy, this being her first shower since they locked her in the room.

Sey-Mi scrubbed her body even after the water ran clear. She washed her hair with the apple-scented shampoo, and then conditioned it. She used a dryer hanging on a hook by the door, then the comb and brush on a shelf beneath it. When she finished, her long, silky hair settled neatly between her shoulders down her back to her hips.

She dressed in a skirt, blouse, and stockings, before slipping on the accompanying pair of high heels. She went up the stairs, the sounds from the outside world greeting her: the rushing of electric busses, the sharp honks from cars, and whines of scooters and roars of motorcycles. More importantly, she heard voices. Real humans speaking, having conversations about things that seemed so far removed from Sey-Mi now. She pushed open a door at the top of the stairs and stepped outside, the night air washing over her. Min Gun stood there staring at her. Though it was faint, she detected the slightest upward curving of his lips as he held his hand out to her.

BUTCHERS

CHAPTER 9

Min Gun struggled to keep his face stoic in the presence of her beauty, but knew he didn't quite succeed, and didn't like the warm emotions threatening to steal over him.

"Welcome back to the world, Kim Sey-Mi." He took her hand in his. "Come with me."

She hesitated a moment, but eventually allowed him to lead her away. She had cleaned up well, the grime from the underground room having been all washed off. Her clothes fit her perfectly. Bought from the upscale Hyundai Department Store, the skirt, blouse and heels had cost hundreds of dollars. Min Gun had picked them out himself. Staring at her now, her face upturned to the night sky high above them, he admitted that he admired Sey-Mi's resolve.

In all the years he'd worked for the *Gwanlyo*, he had never seen a new employee worked over the way Dae Lo had done to Sey-Mi. But then, he had never heard of a new employee catching an experienced member of the organization off guard the way Sey-Mi had. Dae Lo was one of the oldest employees Min Gun had ever met, and his strength and power whelmed those younger than him. Yet Sey-Mi, on only her first day at the job, had slipped through Dae Lo's defenses and torn out his left eye.

Unbeknownst to Sey-Mi, Dae Lo's status had taken a hit in the organization because of the incident. Everyone in the *Gwanlyo* had superiors, and that included Dae Lo. No physical torture would have been as bad as the dressing down he got for such carelessness. And of course, his dressing down had been recorded for all other employees to see. His embarrassment in the eyes of other employees was the worst thing the company could do to him.

So he had taken it out upon Sey-Mi by keeping her in the room far longer than new employees would have been left there. Min Gun quickly realized that Dae Lo had wanted to break her mind. The other employees who he called to help him assaulted her night after night. The perversities they rendered upon her, someone so young and so innocent, were designed to shatter her sense of worth and send her retreating into delusions and ultimately madness.

Despite it all, Sey-Mi had remained steadfast. Min Gun saw it in her eyes after the way they made her groan, grunt, moan and scream with each new obscenity. After each session, her gaze would gradually clear from the fog of pain, and her eyes would shine with hatred. She would then be shackled again and left in the darkness.

"Sey-Mi," Min Gun said, "you have not realized it, but up to this moment, you have been moving too fast for the human world."

Confusion swept Sey-Mi's features. Prepared for that, Min Gun took a phone out of his pocket. "You must remember that you are a member of the *Gwanlyo* now. Your natural movements are those of an employee. From the perspective of a human, every action you take is extraordinary."

He held up the phone before her. "I'm about to let go of your hand, Sey-Mi," he said. "I want you to walk to the end of this street, and then come right back. Go no further than that."

He regretted having to do it, but Min Gun added a threatening tone to his voice. Though he needed to begin teaching her how to control her speed, he couldn't allow her to try to flee. Unknown to Sey-Mi, this was the moment for which Dae Lo waited. He lay in the shadows of the rooftop watching them. He would love nothing more than to see Sey-Mi try and run. He would have to stop her and that would give him a new reason to hurt her.

Min Gun did not want that to happen, and as Sey-Mi regarded him closely, he kept his gaze steady. Finally, she nodded.

"I will come right back," she promised.

I hope you do, Min Gun thought. "I will record your movements and show you afterwards." He released her hand. "Go."

Sey-Mi turned from him and cautiously walked to the end of the street. She paused there and looked to her left and right. Most of the buildings in this neighborhood were run down storage buildings, many of which were owned by the *Gwanlyo*. Sometimes humans found themselves wandering through the narrow alleys, cutting through the buildings, but usually it was empty in this area. That was exactly why the *Gwanlyo* had chosen it for their training grounds. A recent hire was watched closely as they were taught to control their newly gained powers.

Min Gun, watching Sey-Mi, knew she would only get so far if she tried to flee. To his relief, she returned to where he stood. He kept his face neutral and simply held up the phone to her. "Now watch."

Sey-Mi viewed the blur on the phone that materialized into her body when she stopped at the end of the street. Then the blur resumed again until it cleared into her standing before Min Gun once more.

"I don't understand," Sey-Mi gasped out. "How am I doing that?"

"You can't tell right now, but even the words you're speaking are faster than the human ear can distinguish. If they heard us now, it would sound like a string of birdlike whispers spun together. You must truly understand that you are no longer human, Sey-Mi. But to learn how to operate in the world of man starts here." He touched her forehead. "Here you must first envision humanlike behavior. Actions will follow thought.

"Imagine yourself barely moving. Imagine heavy weights around your arms and legs. In your head, see yourself stepping at a snail's pace. Concentrate upon every movement, and separate them. In the human world, you will not move in a continuous flow. Instead, you will move a tiny fraction at a time. A tiny fraction here, a tiny fraction there. That is the only way you can blend in with man."

"Is that possible?" Sey-Mi breathed out. "How can I keep track of so much at the same time?"

"Try," Min Gun urged her. "Close your eyes and attempt it now."

Sey-Mi hesitated, her lack of confidence in his advice evident in her stare. But he spoke no other words, and eventually she inhaled, shut her eyes as he'd instructed, and stood there in silence. Min Gun noticed that she was breathing evenly, and wondered if she realized that she hadn't been doing so regularly since becoming employed in the *Gwanlyo*. Oxygen was inessential for their continued existence, but it did come in handy in blending in and tracking scents. It was also a habit new hires found difficult to break.

Finally, she opened her eyes again.

"Now keep the images you've formed in mind," Min Gun said. "Try again."

Sey-Mi walked to the end of the street and back. This time she managed to move slower, the swing of her arms and the gait of her stride appearing more human. When she returned, Min Gun showed her the video. She had made some improvement in reducing her speed.

"Now again."

For the rest of the night, Sey-Mi practiced moving like a human. Min Gun sensed Dae Lo's frustration in the shadows where he lurked, yet Min Gun knew that next time, Sey-Mi would not be as fortunate. The temptation the *Gwanlyo* placed before new hires proved too much to resist. Only the strongest passed the next test, and when Sey-Mi invariably failed, Dae Lo would have her.

CHAPTER 10

Cheol Yu shook his head in disbelief. "You want to kill a member of the Natural Police?"

Hyeri nodded, a wicked twinkle making her eyes shine. That spark had been setting her gaze on fire lately, and Cheol Yu had become wary in her presence. He didn't ask how she spent her nights when she wasn't there in the apartment with him. He had no intention to join her in killing more humans, but he figured that was exactly the activity she had been engaged in recently.

Hyeri enjoyed laughing, but her laughter masked something dark and cruel. People didn't usually realize until it was too late.

Cheol Yu, however, knew Hyeri well, and asked, "Why take a risk like that?"

They spoke at the normal speed of their kind since they were alone in the apartment. Cheol Yu had just let Hyeri in and was already eyeing her veins. Evening had deepened into night, and the hunger that gnawed at Cheol Yu had become impossible to ignore. He wanted to strip Hyeri and pierce her body at spots that would make her gasp in pleasure, yet Hyeri stood there staring at him, and he knew he would have to hear her out first.

"I don't want to just kill any Natural Police," Hyeri said. "I want to kill the one assigned to watch over your great-grandniece."

"You found her?"

"I know exactly where they're keeping her," she said with a proud nod. "There's a member of the Natural Police who visits her often. There's also *one who punishes* who lurks nearby. He's been going to her less lately. We'll probably have to kill him, too."

She made it sound so simple. Cheol Yu was strong and fast, even for the average employee. The restrictions the *Gwanlyo* placed on them only limited their true potential, but it wasn't uniform in its effect, affecting each of them to different degrees. Cheol Yu had been able to get the upper hand over the two Natural Police who had come to arrest him because of this. If he brawled with agents again, though, they'd be more cautious. Surprising them the first time had been luck. He couldn't count on that a second time.

"So we go and kill the employees," Cheol Yu said. "And then what? We kidnap Sey-Mi…"

"Persuade Sey-Mi," Hyeri interjected.

"And you think she'll just decide to join us?"

"Your great-grandniece will follow you. She liked you, didn't she? She had even decided to spend the night with you."

Cheol Yu had experienced Hyeri's thoughts as he drank from her, but Hyeri also swam through his memories when she drank from him, their bodies clasped together in intimate union. She had seen how close he had come to achieving what he'd wanted from Sey-Mi: her love.

"We'll never get away with it," he said. "You do realize that? We're going to get caught, and if we kill a Natural Police, you never know what the penalty will be. They could actually fire us."

Hyeri sighed. "The *Gwanlyo* doesn't like retiring employees. Do you know how much easier it would be for them to fire us rather than torture us endlessly, only to release us and claim we've been rehabilitated. You ever wonder why?"

It was a good question, Cheol Yu realized. Why did the *Gwanlyo* prefer not to terminate employees? Maybe it was as simple as tradition, passed down over the centuries. Hyeri, born in this modern era, wouldn't understand how important doing what had always been done was to the managers who had been human in a time when that was exactly what kept nations strong. She had no idea how old some of the upper echelons of the organization truly were, and she probably didn't care.

"You have blood on your hands," Hyeri said. "You've already killed an agent of the Natural Police."

"That was in self-defense. The *Gwanlyo* will take that into consideration. What you're proposing is premeditated."

"Maybe that's how you see it, but you don't know if that's how they'll see it," Hyeri countered. "For all you know, they could have already decided to fire you. Honestly, what do you have to lose?"

Hyeri had no proof that the company had come to a decision to retire him. Or did she? Where did she go, and to whom did she speak, when she wasn't in the apartment with him?

Cheol Yu had heard of no one killing an agent of the Natural Police in his many years of employment. Trying to escape them and maiming the agents even Hyeri had done. But Cheol Yu had done more than injure an agent of the Natural Police. He had ripped the heart out of him. Perhaps that crime was unforgivable. If that were the case, would it matter if he killed more agents, then kidnap Sey-Mi and persuade her to join them?

Cheol Yu's shoulders slumped. "So what's this plot of yours? You do have a plan, right?"

"Of course!" Hyeri showed him a video of a neighborhood of old wooden and brick buildings that she had recorded on her phone. "We're going to burn all of this to the ground. We'll start fires at the buildings farthest from where they're keeping Sey-Mi. That should distract any employees who might be in the area. When they try and move Sey-Mi, we'll butcher her escort and take her with us as the *Gwanlyo* deals with the fire and any humans who'll come to the scene. The employees will have their hands too full to notice us."

"We're going to burn these buildings to the ground?"

Hyeri nodded.

"If the fires get out of control and spread, countless humans may die. You can't be serious?"

Hyeri's smile stretched from ear to ear, a Cheshire Cat without a conscience. How much she cared about saving Sey-Mi, and how much she just wanted to engage in wanton destruction, Cheol Yu couldn't determine.

He went to a chair at the table and sat down. Hyeri dropped to a crouch beside him and took his hand, her eyes wide with excitement. He thought about Sey-Mi. Could he bring this upon her? Hyeri didn't seem to mind drawing his great-grandniece into this suicidal scheme, but he did. What did Sey-Mi think about her new job? What were her goals? What had she convinced herself was worth living for when that awful question had been posed to her before she was hired?

Was it fair to take her reason to live death away from her?

Cheol Yu met Hyeri's gaze. "I'm going to have to think about this," he told her. "You have to give me some time to consider the implications of all of this."

"Of course." Hyeri's face almost split apart by her smile. "Take all the time you need."

CHAPTER 11

Min Gun's phone buzzed. He slipped it from his pocket as he exited the subway station, Sey-Mi's newest outfit on a hanger in his hand. He had bought it from Hyundai Department Store the other evening, taking more than an hour to choose the best jeans, cardigan, jacket, and heels for this special day. Sey-Mi had not complained about anything she'd worn over the last several days, but Min Gun hoped she especially liked the items he'd purchased for her today.

When he looked at the name displayed on the phone screen, his eyes narrowed. It was Hyeri.

So far, none of the other employees whom he had visited had gotten back to him with information about Cheol Yu. Of all the individuals he had approached, Hyeri was the last one he thought would have information to pass on to him. Even if she discovered something about Cheol Yu's whereabouts, he didn't expect her to willingly divulge it to the *Gwanlyo*.

Staring at her name, Min Gun considered the best way to speak with her, then pressed the phone icon. "You called."

"I did what you asked me to if I found something out." She sounded hesitant, which piqued Min Gun's interest.

"I wasn't sure what to do," Hyeri continued. "Cheol Yu called. He needs help, and wants to meet me."

"Where?"

"I don't know yet. Probably somewhere private, away from human eyes." She inhaled. "I remember how strong Cheol Yu was. If he finds out that I betrayed him, he'll butcher me alive. I know it."

Her concerns weren't unwarranted. Min Gun's superior, Jun Young, had been one of the *Gwanlyo*'s best agents. Cheol Yu had still managed to push through the restraints placed upon him, murder Jun Young, and escape.

"He won't harm you," Min Gun told Hyeri as images of Cheol Yu ripping out Jun Young's heart flashed through his thoughts. "The *Gwanlyo* will protect you. Your cooperation in this matter will be highly regarded in the organization. Your status is set to rise if this operation to capture Cheol Yu is successfully completed."

Hyeri sighed with relief. "That's all I really want, to be back in the good graces of the organization. I will contact you again in a day or two when Cheol Yu sets a meeting place. Will that work for you?"

Min Gun nodded. "That will be perfect. Until then, Hyeri."

Min Gun ended the call and continued to the building where Sey-Mi was kept. He went downstairs into the basement and placed the outfit on the hook by the bathroom. Every day he breathed a mental sigh of relief that the locked metal door was still closed. He wasn't sure if Sey-Mi realized that she could force it open if she wanted. But then, the monitors would pick that up and instantly alert the nearby Dae Lo, who would take great pleasure in hunting her down and bring her back here.

Min Gun unlocked the door and stepped into the dark room. They no longer kept Sey-Mi bound, and she wore clothes now. Min Gun had brought her a mat so she would not have to sleep on the dirty floor. Right now, she sat cross-legged and stared at him as he approached. Disappointment flooded her face when her eyes dropped to his hand and she saw he did not carry the bottle of blood.

Min Gun did not address its absence. "Today we will start a new lesson. Please take a shower and dress."

She stood and began to take off her clothes. Min Gun turned away and went back upstairs to wait for her. She emerged minutes later in the slim blue jeans and a bright red jacket over the cream cardigan. Her hair fell straight down between her shoulders to her hips. Despite everything Dae Lo had put her through, innocence still brightened her features and gave Sey-Mi a girlish glow as she stared with wide eyes at Min Gun.

"Come with me," he said. She placed her hand in his and they walked away from the basement with their shoulders touching. Her fingers were petite wrapped around his, her flesh cold because she had not fed yet.

"Sey-Mi," Min Gun said quietly, "I am going to reintroduce you to the world of humans tonight."

Her grasp tightened around his. Min Gun remembered the first time he had been sent back out among the humans after being hired by the *Gwanlyo*. It had terrified him, not because of what humans could do to him, but because of what he might do to them if he did not maintain control. The same thoughts probably ran through Sey-Mi's mind.

The smells of nearby restaurants greeted them: the sweet baking of bread, the salty aroma of pizza, the meaty whiff of grilling galbi. They walked narrow alleys past windowless buildings. The sound of traffic, of barreling busses and cars rushing down streets, and the sharp honks of taxis, echoed around them. Soon, conversations floated in the air: complaints about bosses, worries about grades, the shrieks of playing children and the exhausted calls of parents trying to corral them.

Finally, they turned a corner and stepped into a tide of humans. Sey-Mi took a sharp breath and stepped forward hesitantly. Min Gun immediately noticed male eyes lingering upon her as they passed. Like all *Gwanlyo* employees, Sey-Mi had grown more attractive, more alluring. But Min Gun saw something else in her, too. Beneath that innocence was incredible strength, a bright spirit that lit up the dark world of the *Gwanlyo*. Min Gun wanted to experience it for himself, and fought against a rising desire to pull her into the shadows and pierce her throat.

Sey-Mi would not have noticed during the ordeal that Dae Lo and the other men put her through in the basement, but even they had not forced themselves upon her in that most intimate acts for employees. No one fed upon another employee without that person's permission, even during severe torture. To do so was a taboo instinctively shared among all who joined the organization, so that there was no known punishment for any who broke it.

Eventually, Min Gun led her to a building with a red, white, and blue pole rotating above its door. 'Bright Flower Massage' was printed on a sign with the silhouette of a naked girl. He led Sey-Mi up steps lit red to the second floor, a bell announcing their arrival ringing once above their heads.

"The *Gwanlyo* owns businesses like this around the city," he explained to her. "Karaokes, *noraebangs*, bars, clubs, gambling houses. Places humans visit at night to lose themselves in vice. These establishments are useful for us, not only because of the revenue they bring in, but also because they allow for quick feeds without having to hunt humans in a world filled with CCTV and hand phones constantly filming everything."

They stepped through an automatic door into a cool, dimly lit lobby. A middle-aged woman sitting behind a counter stood and bowed to Min Gun.

"You messaged that you have a customer waiting?" he asked her. She nodded.

"I shared some whiskey with him while he waited," she said. "He asked for the company of a girl." She looked Sey-Mi up and down. "He will be very pleased with her."

Min Gun struggled against a sudden feeling that he tried to identify. Was it annoyance? Frustration? Why did the thought of this man touching Sey-Mi darken his mood? He didn't want to see the look in her face at the revelation of what she must now do, but he didn't have a choice in this matter. They were employees of the *Gwanlyo*, and she must learn to feed.

"Go to him and tell him that a girl has arrived," Min Gun told the woman. "She will join him in a moment."

The woman bowed and went down the narrow hall. Min Gun turned to Sey-Mi and maintained a neutral expression when he saw the revulsion on her face. "You will go to this man," he said without emotion, "and you will pierce his neck here." He touched the vein in the side of her throat. "You will drink from him, but you must not kill him. This is very important, Sey-Mi." Min Gun added the threatening tone to his voice that he had used with her before. The way she flinched darkened his mood further, but he knew Dae Lo was nearby hoping that Sey-Mi failed tonight.

"We do not kill humans." Min Gun slipped a cold, foreboding mask over his face and loomed over her. "It is forbidden. We are powerful, but we are few. If the mortal world ever discovers our existence, we will be destroyed. This truth has been foretold since the beginning."

Min Gun watched with satisfaction as fear completely swept her revulsion away. She cast a desperate look down the hall. "What am I supposed to do?" She stepped towards him. "Can't you come with me?"

Min Gun stilled his arms from wrapping around her. Stepping away, he shook his head. "I cannot. You must do this on your own. Drink from him, but I repeat, do not kill him."

The door at the end of the hall opened. The woman stepped back out and motioned to Sey-Mi.

"Now go, Sey-Mi, and do your job."

CHAPTER 12

Sey-Mi searched Min Gun's face, but it remained blank. Surely he didn't expect her to go into the room at the end of the hall alone. And once she was with the strange man, what should she do? Allow him to touch her? To undress her? To do more?

After everything the men had done to her against her will, the very thought of what awaited in that room not only disgusted her, but also angered her. Right now, she didn't know what she would do if another man tried to force himself upon her. Min Gun's warning settled heavily around her shoulders. She could not kill the man. The punishment, he had hinted, would be most severe. Sey-Mi didn't want to ponder what that entailed.

The woman went behind the counter and stared expectantly at Sey-Mi. Sey-Mi inhaled to capture the woman's scent. Beneath the flowery perfume, Sey-Mi picked up the unmistakable aroma of blood. The sharp iron smell made the hunger inside of her twist, warping her thoughts so that she found focusing difficult. She must feed, and her meal was at the end of the hall.

Sey-Mi started down the tiled hall, her gaze never straying from the closed door. She had never stepped into a massage parlor before, but she had seen their signs. The swirling poles alongside buildings designating places where men could find the company of women for a price dotted alleys throughout Seoul.

Sey-Mi didn't remember when she became aware of what went on inside of these establishments. Maybe middle school? But she knew that good girls like her didn't end up working in places like this. Her parents had raised her in a nice apartment and had sent her to one of the best schools in Seoul. They had always planned for her to go to one of the top universities, work in an office until she got married, and then have kids.

What would her parents think now if they saw her in these expensive clothes in this massage parlor, a man waiting for her at the end of the hall?

Sey-Mi stumbled, and reached out to steady herself on the wall. Images of her parents flashed in her thoughts. For the briefest moment, the grief that swelled up inside of her swallowed the hunger. How long had it been since she had disappeared from their lives? Did they think she had died? Were the Seoul Metropolitan Police searching for her?

She was sure that her mom and dad would have alerted the authorities the very night she didn't return home. Would she ever see her family again? Could she look her mother and father in the eye after all Dae Lo and the other men had done to her? The shame would be unbearable, and now here she was going to the arms of yet another man. Why had this terrible fate befallen her? What had she done to deserve this?

The hunger would not stay buried beneath her grief for long. It erupted through her fiercer than before as if cursing her hesitation. *Don't think of your parents,* it whispered. *I am the center of your universe. You belong to me.*

Sey-Mi licked her lips and continued down the hall. The hunger sucked up her decency, her longing, her steadfast determination to see her parents again. Until it was satisfied, nothing else existed. She must do what she had to in order to survive. She must honor the pact she made to become an employee of the *Gwanlyo*. She could do nothing else now. Finally standing in front of the door at the end of the hall, she took a deep breath and knocked softly.

"Come in," a male voice said. Sey-Mi gripped the knob, gently turned it, and stepped inside.

The man sat on a chair beside a long massage table, a small bottle of whiskey and a bucket of ice in an alcove. His fingers rested on a glass with a thumb of golden liquor in it. Another glass had melting ice, and the last was empty.

The man's eyes widened as he looked Sey-Mi up and down. "How old are you?" Suspicion laced his question, and he sat back from her.

Realizing she couldn't say seventeen, Sey-Mi replied, "Twenty."

The lie came easily, surprising her. Other than small falsehoods to her parents and teachers, Sey-Mi usually told the truth. She had had little reason to do otherwise in her ideal life. Not until she met Cheol Yu and felt she had fallen in love was she prepared to lie about something important so she could spend the night with him.

"You look young." The man looked at the door. "Are you really here for me? Maybe there is a mistake."

She couldn't let him leave this room without finishing her task. She imagined women she'd seen on television enticing guys, and pulled her face into a smile in perfect imitation of those actresses. She slid off her jacket, slowly revealing her body, turned, and placed the jacket on a hook fastened to the wall. She took her time so that the man could see her from behind, then faced him again. His hungry eyes were on her body. She sensed the battle warring inside of him. He didn't believe she was twenty, but how much could he make himself care?

"I can get you another girl," Sey-Mi said, "but I would love to spend some time with you." She stepped to the massage table and leaned her hip against the dark leather. "Would you like to spend more time with me?"

The man's breathing quickened, his gaze continually appraising her hips, her chest, her legs, her face. He wore nothing but a white robe, his clothes already neatly folded on a shelf by the shower door. The bulge growing beneath the robe won out against his doubts. Sey-Mi raised her hands to him, and he stood and gently grasped her fingers. He was several centimeters taller than she was and seemed to be in his 40s. She smelled whiskey and mints on his breath when he leaned in closer to her and said, "You must be cold from outside. You're freezing."

Sey-Mi didn't know how to respond, so she untied his robe and slid it off him. Leaning past him so that their bodies briefly touched, she draped the robe carefully on the chair. The musk of his excitement filled the air, his palms resting on her sides.

"Lie down," she said, indicating the table, "and I'll run hot water over my hands."

She went into the shower and turned on the faucet until steam misted the mirror. She let water run over her flesh until it stung, and then went back to him hoping he would no longer notice a chill to her skin. The man lay on his stomach. Sey-Mi briefly considered his naked body. She had never given a massage before and had no idea how she should do it. She had seen woman give men massages on television programs, and once again, she decided to mimic them.

Sey-Mi reached for a folded towel under the massage table, opened it to its full length, and laid it over the man so that it stretched from his neck to his ankles. Then she placed her hands on his back. He stiffened under her touch. She pressed down on the muscles along his hips, moved up his sides to his shoulders. After she slid her hands down the complete length of his body, his muscles relaxed.

She pulled the towel down to his hips to expose his back and reached for a bottle of almond oil next to the massage table. She poured the yellowish substance into her cupped palm and let it trickle onto his flesh. She rubbed the oil into his shoulders, biceps, and down his sides. The man's breathing slowed as Sey-Mi's excitement grew. The metallic aroma of his blood wafted up from him, and a pleasurable tingle in her incisors forced all other thoughts from her mind as her need for blood blossomed. She kept kneading his skin as she leaned in closer to him. Her face hovered over his neck; she inhaled deeply, and brought her lips to his throat in a kiss that pierced his jugular.

The man gasped sharply. His muscles clenched in ecstasy that Sey-Mi shared with him. Fire burned through them. Sey-Mi sucked on the wound harder, her mouth locked to his flesh as blood spurted across her tongue. Fragmented memories from the man poured into her as she fed: his son doing compulsory service in the army; his daughter in high school; his wife tending their home; his work at a small business trading and selling goods; his staff and their daily routine; his boredom at married life, at being an adult with numerous responsibilities giving rise to an itch for moments of excitement. The massage parlors he visited to meet willing girls scratched that itch.

Sey-Mi even saw his thoughts on her, the youngest girl he'd met in one of these establishments. She saw his desire conflicted within him since he wanted to protect her innocence but, more strongly, he wanted to ravish her purity.

Only a little more, a voice inside of Sey-Mi warned, *not too much, pull back gently or lose yourself completely.* She struggled against its advice but managed to push herself away from the man. The puncture wounds were smaller than she had imagined, tiny rivulets of blood snaking down his neck to his collar. She bent and licked it away. The wound closed as her tongue passed over it so that only two red pinpoints remained.

The man had been left dazed, his breathing shallow, his pallor pale. Sey-Mi worried that she had taken too much from him. Gently she shook his shoulder. "I'm all done," she said into his ear. "You can get up now."

The man opened his eyes and stared blankly at her for several moments. Clearing his throat, he allowed her to help him sit up and motioned to the chair. "Please, hand me my robe."

Sey-Mi steadied him as he stood, and helped him into the robe. He sat down at the table and poured two fingers of whiskey into his glass. Checking the time on his phone, he said, "I think you can stay with me for a few minutes more. Join me for a drink."

Sey-Mi glanced at the door. She didn't know how long the man had rented her company, but she didn't want to upset him with everything going so smoothly. She pictured the models she saw in advertisements and pulled one of their smiles onto her face. She sat down across from him and rested a hand on his exposed thigh.

"You're warm now." He poured a finger of whisky into the empty glass and slid it towards her. "I can't say the same for me."

Sey-Mi arched her eyebrows and offered him a demure nod in response. His gaze locked onto her face, and he said in obvious awe, "You really are beautiful. I will give you my card. Call me. A night with me will be worth your while."

"Thank you." Sey-Mi took his card. "Now let's drink before our time is done."

"Yes." The man held up his glass, and she followed suit. The golden liquor sparkled in the ice. Sey-Mi had drunk beer and soju before, but never whiskey. She watched the man take a thirsty gulp. Sey-Mi imitated him, placing the glass to her lips and upending the liquor in one shot.

The taste of rot exploded into her mouth. Reflexively, Sey-Mi spewed the whiskey out of her mouth onto the floor. The man sat back, surprised. Sey-Mi struggled to hold down the nausea sweeping through her. Was this supposed to taste so terrible? Embarrassment flooded her, and she wiped away the strands of salvia dripping down her chin. She glanced at the man expecting him to be horrified. Instead, his surprise turned to laughter. He grabbed a towel and wiped off her lips. “You really are young.” He laughed as he dabbed at her lips. “I think this is the first time you ever had alcohol.”

Sey-Mi didn’t respond. If she spoke, she would vomit, and he wouldn’t find that funny at all. He drew closer to her. Sey-Mi’s hunger, which she thought was sated, shook itself awake and roiled her senses. The man rested a hand on her side, then slid it up to her chest to cup her breast. His lips hovered near hers, then pressed upon them. His tongue pushed into her mouth. For moments he kissed her, then he pulled back to kiss her cheek, then under her ear. Again, Sey-Mi’s lips brushed his neck. Her incisors extended against her will. For the second time that night, she pierced his throat. His body tightened as the fire tore through them again. This time, the voice that warned her to stop became quiet. She drank from him, crushing his body to hers.

The massage door flung open. Min Gun darted into the room and grabbed Sey-Mi’s shoulder. She leapt from him to the wall, the man in her arms.

“I can’t stop them if you kill him,” Min Gun hissed. “I won’t be able to help you next time!”

Images of Dae Lo flooded her mind. With a growl, Sey-Mi let the man drop onto the table, and he rolled off to hit the floor. Min Gun crouched next to him and placed his hand to the man’s throat. Another voice at the door broke the moment of silence. Both Sey-Mi and Min Gun turned to Dae Lo standing there.

“Did she kill him?”

Min Gun shook his head. “He’ll live, but he’s weak. He won’t be going anywhere anytime soon.”

Dae Lo looked at Sey-Mi clinging to the wall and said to Min Gun, “Her next lesson will be with me. It seems she still has a far way to go before she can assume a proper role in the *Gwanlyo*.

“Dream new memories into this man about this encounter.” And then he was gone.

CHAPTER 13

Sey-Mi flinched when the lock turned in the metal door. Dae Lo entered the basement. She didn't want to show weakness in front of him, but she went rigid despite the fact that he displayed no outward hostility towards her. He carried a new outfit on a hanger in a plastic bag, and a pair of boots.

"Dress quickly," he told her. "We have a lot to accomplish tonight."

He didn't turn away as Min Gun had, so Sey-Mi undressed in front of him. He didn't step aside when she passed him to the shower in the next room, his gaze steady upon her. She read in his posture the conviction that he possessed her body and could do with it what he wanted. And she could tell he wanted to do so much to her. Dae Lo didn't have to touch her to make her feel violated. It was all there in his eyes.

When she had dried off, she pulled on the red silk underwear and bra, the leggings, gray plaid skirt and cashmere sweater. She wrapped a colorful scarf around her neck, slid on the light green jacket and the knee high black boots. Min Gun would have expressed appreciation in the way she wore the outfit. Dae Lo's stare, on the other hand, was a blunt object filled with violence. He wanted to hurt her. He wanted to make her scream.

"Follow me."

He turned and went back up the stairs. She followed him, and they stepped out into a cold night. The clear sky boasted a full moon that hung low in the horizon over Seoul. It was early, a little after six. When they exited the twisting alleys leading past the quiet buildings, they stepped into the bustling city streets. Dae Lo didn't hold her hand as Min Gun had, and she was glad of it. Yet she wished Min Gun were there to act as her anchor as she walked past the humans. Her hunger stormed inside of her, her incisor teeth tingling at the smell of blood in the air. She ached to pull someone warm close to her, to pierce their throat and drink that which made her feel whole, made her feel alive. The desire bloomed, threatening to rip her apart. Her body tensed as she ground her teeth in her struggle to maintain control.

Dae Lo must have sensed her internal conflict, but he said nothing, offering no words of solace to keep her strong. When he stopped, Sey-Mi was unfocused and bumped against him. They stood in front of a Café Bene, and she looked at the coffee chain in confusion.

"I can tell that you're hungry." He opened the door. "Come; let's rest here for a while."

The Café Bene was crowded. Students bent over textbooks and scribbled in notepads. Young workers chatted amongst themselves while couples leaned in towards each other in intimate conversation. K-pop showered down from speakers, infusing the atmosphere with energy.

Sey-Mi walked beside Dae Lo to the counter. She stared at the assortments of ice creams, cakes, and pastries behind the display case, and thought back to times when she and her friends had a little extra spending money. They would pool their resources and stop at a Café Bene between school and private tutoring, ordering an assortment of foods and caffeinated drinks. They would arrange the plates on a large table and share a private feast while they traded gossip and complaints about high school life.

Fond memories washed over her until Dae Lo said, "Order whatever you want. It's on me."

Normally, a phrase like that would be spoken in kindness. Dae Lo's voice remained cold and dripped with venom. Sey-Mi stared at the extensive menu above the heads of the employees, but none of her favorite desserts attracted her now. In fact, the very idea of consuming human food held no appeal.

"I'm not hungry," she said to Dae Lo. "I'll just sit down with you while you eat."

"It wasn't a request," he said, and she sensed the violent surge threatening to spill out of him. "You will eat here."

She realized that he knew exactly what she was thinking. He hadn't brought her here on a whim. This was a plan, another test to see how she handled herself in this crowded coffee house. Sey-Mi glanced around at the humans going about their daily lives, and terror spiked through her.

Dae Lo was waiting for her to fail so that he could enact some new torture upon her. She swallowed her terror, but it would not go away. She should run, but Dae Lo's stance was poised, ready. He wanted her to try to escape.

She wouldn't give Dae Lo the opportunity he sought. If she was going to fail, she would go down fighting.

It was their turn now, and the two of them stepped up to the counter. The male server stared openly at her, and it took a moment before he breathlessly said, "Welcome to Café Bene." A flush touched his cheek. Clearing his throat, he added, "Will you be dining here this evening?"

He gazed at her the same way the man in the massage parlor had. Would she inspire this reaction in all men? Before the *Gwanlyo* hired her, she received little attention from boys. She attended an all-girls school where the only males she saw were teachers who paid her the same level of attention as they did every other girl in the school. When studying after school at hagwons or cafes with her friends, she had been indistinguishable from every other teen girl. But now?

She held the server's eyes. He leaned towards her and reddened further. Her gaze slid to his neck, her hunger a siren enchanting her with its music. She longed to reach out to the male before her, caress his cheek, run her fingers down the side of his face to his throat and slice open his jugular so that his blood flowed freely down his collar. She would lap it away with the tip of her tongue, drawing out the moment before she placed her lips against the wound and sucked out the liquid nourishment she craved.

Her hand rose towards him. Out of the corner of her eye, she noticed Dae Lo. If it had been Min Gun, he would have said something to wake her from her bloodlust. Dae Lo, however, just stood there staring as hungrily at her as she did at the server before her. Sey-Mi dropped her hand to her side and looked beyond the server to the menu behind him.

"A black sugar latte." Her voice sounded strained in her ears. "And a plain bagel."

She hadn't eaten anything since that night long ago in Cheol Yu's apartment. She hoped a simple bagel would be easier to digest. She wasn't even sure how her new body would react to food. Since she had been hired by the *Gwanlyo*, she hadn't had the urge to go to the bathroom. She hadn't had her monthly period. This body felt artificial, reconstructed when she hadn't been paying attention.

The server turned to Dae Lo. "And you, sir?"

Dae Lo stepped forward. "A caramel macchiato, to begin with."

Sey-Mi turned to him.

"We would also like a large red bean pat-bing-su, a green tea bagel, and a sweet potato bagel."

The server rang up the order while Sey-Mi's hands clenched nervously. Did Dae Lo really expect her to eat all of that?

After he paid, she followed him to the dining area. She saw an empty booth near the rear of the room and hoped he would go there. Dae Lo instead went to a table in the center of the coffee house and motioned for Sey-Mi to sit down. She stared at the chair as the voices of the customers washed over her. She would have to face this test head on. Pulling back the seat, she sat down. Dae Lo sat down opposite her.

Laughter from a group of girls floated through the dining area. Across from Sey-Mi, a couple sat on the same side of a booth, their heads close together, their hands touching as they talked. She envied the humans around her enjoying each other's company. Unlike her with a dining companion who hated her.

Sey-Mi thought back to the night they first met. She'd been terrified of what would happen to her in that dark room. When Dae Lo slammed her head into the concrete to get her to pay attention to the video, all she wanted to do was escape before he harmed her further.

So when the opportunity presented itself, when the unlocked chains fell from her wrists and ankles, she had attacked. His eye seemed the easiest target, and she had surprised herself with how much damage she rendered upon him when she ripped it out of his face. She didn't hesitate as he cried out in pain. She bolted to the door to throw it open to freedom. Then the shadowy men poured into the room and caught her. For many days after that, those men and Dae Lo assaulted her without pity. She had screamed, she had pleaded, but no one came to her rescue. She was at their mercy.

As she sat in the café before Dae Lo's unbridled hatred now, she wondered if things could have gone differently if she hadn't attacked him. She wished that her initial interaction with Dae Lo could start over again, but a larger part of her admitted another truth. Every time she looked at him, every time she heard his voice, she remembered what he did to her during those long nights of pain and suffering. The memories filled her with barely suppressed rage. She knew that she would never be able to quell her desire to make him suffer as he had made her suffer.

She wanted to kill Dae Lo. She simply waited for the best opportunity to do so.

The buzzer the cashier had given Dae Lo rang. He went to the counter and came back with a tray filled with plates. He placed it on the table between them, then sat down again. Sey-Mi's stomach twisted at the sight of it. She noticed customers glance at their large order in surprise. Not only was she in the center of the room, but she also had an audience. Worry suffused her as nausea made her mouth water with saliva.

"I have some news to give you, but we should eat some first." He handed her a spoon. "You are to begin now."

CHAPTER 14

Hyeri struggled to keep the smile off her face as she keyed in a message to the Natural Police. What was his name? Min Gun?

Seated across from her in the Hyehwa apartment, Cheol Yu stared at a televised concert. One of Korea's biggest K-pop groups had travelled to New York City. The local stations were playing a repeat of their performance.

"Hyeri." Cheol Yu turned to her at a commercial break. "It's time I left Korea."

Hyeri stopped tapping on the Smartphone and read what she'd written: *He's here. Come immediately!* She added a ping for their location, pressed the arrow icon to send it, and laid her phone on the table. Then she met Cheol Yu's gaze.

"What about Sey-Mi?" She struggled to bury the smile. Cheol Yu would be surprised when he discovered that she had taken matters into her own hands.

"I can't fight the *Gwanlyo*." He leaned back, defeat etched into his features. "There's just too many of them. No matter how much I want to get her, I'm just one person."

"One person?" The laugh pushed up against her gut into her throat. "But I'm here to help you. You don't need anyone but me."

"Hyeri." Cheol Yu sighed. "I don't think your plan will work. It's too dangerous. Setting fire to a neighborhood in Seoul to smoke out the employees watching Sey-Mi? That'll draw too much attention from the mortal world."

Her phone buzzed, and Hyeri read the message: *We're on our way.* To Cheol Yu, she said, "That's why the plan's brilliant! The more humans that get involved, the less likely the *Gwanlyo* can use their full powers to stop us from taking Sey-Mi. They'll be too worried about being discovered."

Cheol Yu bit the bottom of his lip. "I don't know. It's just so risky."

Hyeri couldn't hold it back any longer. Peals of laughter danced out from between her parted lips. *"But that's why I'm here!"*

Her shriek resonated in the apartment. Cheol Yu tensed, a myriad of emotions warring across his face.

"Hyeri!" He grasped her shoulders. "What have you done?"

"What I had to! You're standing at the edge and just need a good push." She raised her phone and showed him the message. "So now I'm going to shove you over."

Cheol Yu read the text and frowned. "Who's coming?"

Her smile was so wide it felt like it was consuming her face. "They're coming! The *Gwanlyo*, the Natural Police. Your hunters, all coming, here!"

Realization slowly dawned in Cheol Yu's eyes. A look of horror swiftly followed. "You didn't. Hyeri, tell me you didn't!"

"Would I lie to you?" A fresh round of laughter exploded from Hyeri. Cheol Yu pounced to his feet, and Hyeri immediately blocked him.

"These are your options," she howled through her laughter. "Stay here and fight the organization, or go to Sey-Mi and fight the organization. The choice is yours!"

Hyeri snatched up the shoulder bag she had prepared with brake fluid and chlorine, dashed to the window and threw it open. "They'll be here any minute! Take them on with me, or take them on alone!"

She grabbed the window edge and flung herself outside to the rough brick wall. She scaled up the side of the building to the rooftop and scanned the area. Cheol Yu was beside her in an instant.

"Damn you, Hyeri!"

Hyeri grabbed Cheol Yu and pointed. He followed her gaze to two Natural Police clinging to the side of a wall opposite them, their butchering tools hanging from straps around their bodies. She recognized Min Gun and waved. Then she spun away, darted across the rooftop, leapt to the next building, then the next in the direction of Banghwa. She had fed from several victims tonight so she would have sufficient power to tap into when needed. The blood pumped through her heart and burned in her veins as s he pushed herself to top speeds to put distance between herself and the Natural Police. She had to get to her secret stash before they could stop her.

Over the last several nights, Hyeri had been stealing bottles of brake fluid from automotive garages, and liters of powdered chlorine from hardware stores. She stored them in the electronic shop that had belonged to the man with the golden watch. Last night, she had situated them, as well as two dozen butane flasks, around the neighborhood where the *Gwanlyo* kept Sey-Mi. Once she reached them, she would spread the chlorine along the rooftops and pour the brake fluid over the white powder. The resulting poisonous chemical fires would distract the employees and keep the humans busy while Cheol Yu rescued Sey-Mi.

The gray man of smoke and shadows loomed in her thoughts. The world had ignored her once while she suffered. It was only fair that she returned the favor.

CHAPTER 15

I will not vomit, Sey-Mi repeated to herself. She reached out and picked up the warm mug of black sugar latte. Once one of her favorite drinks, she used to order it when studying with her friends. A part of her wished her girlfriends were sitting with her now. But then, that would expose them to the monster sitting across from her. She wouldn't want Dae Lo to have access to anyone she ever held dear in her old life.

Sey-Mi raised the mug to her lips and took a sip of the latte. The hot liquid sat in her mouth and refused to go down. She focused on her tongue, which didn't want her to swallow. It was sending waves of disgust to her throat, which was refusing to take the latte to her stomach. Yet Dae Lo stared at her, unblinking, a gleam in his eyes. Sey-Mi swished the latte around in her mouth, focused on ignoring its rotten taste, and finally swallowed. Her body shivered at the invasion of noxious liquid, but she kept it from surging back up.

"Delicious." She tried to speak in a steady voice but the word came out as a strangled gasp. The glow in Dae Lo's eyes brightened at the misery he inflicted. He had looked the same as he assaulted her those many nights, inserting objects into any part of her that would take it. Worse still was when he forced himself inside of her, with his body slapping against hers as he brutally thrust into her. He would put his face directly over hers as she begged him for mercy. But he desired pure agony from her as if he fed upon her screams.

Dae Lo slid the bagel to her. "More."

Sey-Mi stared at the round bread for a moment before reaching for it.

"First," Dae Lo said. He picked up the small container of cream cheese, opened the bagel and speared copious amounts of the thick white substance on one half, then the other, before putting them back together. "Now it's ready."

He stared at her as she reached for it. Even before she bit into it, she gagged. There would be no getting out of it, so she took a small bite. The latte had been difficult to swallow, but that was liquid. Chewing the bread kept the revolting taste of food in her mouth longer. She struggled to maintain a blank expression on her face, fought to work the bagel in saliva as the cream cheese coated her teeth. Dae Lo never took his eyes off her. The sounds of other people in the restaurant kept her aware of the presence of humans as she struggled to do what was once natural.

She got it down, but the rest of the bagel was like a weight in her hand, and she still had to finish the latte. This was going to be impossible, yet Dae Lo's desire to see her fail motivated her to soldier on until her body finally gave in and vomited up what she could not keep down.

Dae Lo dished out some of the *pat-bing-su* into a small bowl and started to eat. He spooned up the mixture of fresh fruit, corn chips, red beans, and ice chips, and neatly scooped it into his mouth. He took several deep gulps of his caramel macchiato, the expression on his face never changing as he consumed the human food. Sey-Mi couldn't help but be amazed at how effortlessly he did this, and she wondered if there was something fundamentally different about him from her. When she took another drink of the black sugar latte, and another bite of the bagel, the task became more difficult, not easier. Seconds aged into minutes. The first bagel finished, the latte drank, Sey-Mi's stomach revolting against her, she shuddered when Dae Lo pushed the green tea bagel in front of her.

A half hour of misery passed. The food Sey-Mi had eaten bubbled up into her throat, and she repeatedly swallowed to push it back down. Dae Lo quickly finished his serving and removed an envelope from his pocket.

"Now to other business." He took several sheets of paper from the envelope and put them on the table before her. The first one was a rental agreement for an apartment in Shinchon.

"The *Gwanlyo* has authorized a new apartment for you. You will move there at the end of the week." He tapped the address printed on the paper, then flipped the page to a bank account. "This will be your private savings account. Every month an allowance will be placed into it. Charges will be carefully scrutinized. The company is generous with its employees, but they will not tolerate waste."

Sey-Mi stopped chewing. Soggy food sat at the base of her mouth as she stared at the documents before her. He couldn't be serious. Sey-Mi looked at Dae Lo for signs of a cruel joke he was pulling on her, but she saw no hints of that. The *Gwanlyo* was giving her an apartment? And a monthly stipend? She tried to swallow, but the food she had already consumed kept rising, and she clamped her lips shut.

"And now, this."

Dae Lo flipped to the next page. She noticed a change in his demeanor. Something about what he would say next disturbed him. He was reluctant to reveal this new information, but she realized that he had no choice. For the first time, Sey-Mi sensed something akin to fear radiating from her tormentor.

"Sey-Mi, the *Gwanlyo* has carefully reviewed your case and has decided you are to become a member of the Natural Police." He produced a pen from his pocket and placed it on the table next to the papers. "Read these carefully and sign your name on each page."

Sey-Mi stared at the pen. She instructed her hand to reach out to it, but it did not obey her. She sent it another directive, and her hand slowly lifted and picked up the pen. The Natural Police? Min Gun had mentioned that he belonged to the same group. The *Gwanlyo* wanted her to catch bad guys? Did they think that highly of her?

Sey-Mi tried to read the first page about her duties but found it difficult to concentrate on the words swirling in her vision. Her hands shook as she touched the point of the pen to the line at the bottom and signed it. A slight tingling affected the tips of her fingers and zipped up along her arm to spread throughout her body. Reality went up a notch. Voices in the café became louder, sharper, clearer. The hum of tires against asphalt outside reached her, the echo of high heels on concrete and even the distant roar of planes were detected by her increased hearing. The aroma of coffees and lattes grew overpowering, the cinnamon scent of baked breads and sweet icing layering themselves over her. The crisp winter temperature lingering in the warm indoor air fought for dominance on the surface of her skin. The tiny fibers of the document stood out on the white paper so that she had to blink several times to make sense of what lay before her.

"Restriction one, released," Dae Lo said.

Sey-Mi wanted to look at him, but realized the speed with which she would do so would have been inhumanly fast. Instead, she slowly dragged her eyes up in imitation of the humans around her and stared at Dae Lo. His hatred for her stood out even clearer than before and pierced her to her core.

"Continue," he instructed her.

It took several breaths for her to untangle herself from the raw vehemence dripping from the three syllables of that single word he uttered and flip to the second page. A list of violations crowded together here, so many tiny threats marching from one end of the margin to the other. Too caught up in this new world of sights, sounds and smells to comprehend their individual meanings, she skipped them and signed her name again. The tingling became a spark, a live wire rushing through her as reality went up another octave.

Why did he do this here, in this public place surrounded by humans? And yet Sey-Mi knew the answer, knew he had planned this with the desperate hope that she would not be able to tame this incredible fine-tuning of her sensory perception. Worst of all, the smell of blood, always emanating from mortals, crystallized so clear that she could detect health, age and sex of the humans sitting around her. Her incisors throbbed, and she struggled against their lengthening which might force her to part her lips holding back the contents of her stomach.

The next pages of the document stated punishments. These seemed to go on without end, the lettering growing tiny in the fine print. Have they thought of everything, Sey-Mi wondered, and shuddered at the second thought: have they tried everything?

Sey-Mi signed her name on the last page, slid the contract to Dae Lo, turned from him, and opened her mouth. Everything she'd just consumed came back up in a torrent of undigested food that splattered on the café floor.

CHAPTER 16

Dae Lo affixed his face into one of utmost concern as he watched Sey-Mi spit out the food she'd been unable to keep down. Inside, he laughed, long and with dark satisfaction. His pleasure at her public failure almost distorted the mask he needed to maintain as patrons turned in shocked surprise to their table. He had successfully made Sey-Mi fail in front of humans, and he would be able to punish her again. He longed to see how she reacted to the torture he had planned this time.

Dae Lo collected the signed documents in the envelope and put it back in his pocket. The server rushed over to them, his eyes darting to the other customers as he hovered over Sey-Mi. "I'm so sorry," he said. "Is she okay?"

Dae Lo waved him aside. "She hasn't been feeling well all week." He crouched beside Sey-Mi and held back her long hair. Soon they would be alone in the basement, and her silky black hair would be wound tight in his fingers as he yanked back on her head. He would pull so hard that it would rip out in bloody clumps from her scalp.

"Do you need me to call anyone?" The server had positioned himself in such a way to shield the patrons from the undigested food on the floor.

Dae Lo shook his head as he helped Sey-Mi to her feet. "I'll take good care of her," he promised the young man. Sey-Mi's face twisted in horror. Again, his inner laugh threatened to break the mask of concern, especially at her expression of terror, which he would amplify soon. He could not let the humans notice her reaction, however, and he put her arm around his shoulder and quickly went to the door. When she hesitated, he took her hand and bent her thumb back slightly to make her exhale in pain.

"Remember the papers you just signed," he whispered to her. "Remember the violations and punishments for exposing the *Gwanlyo* to humans. You've done enough already. Will you take it further?"

Sey-Mi glanced back at the humans in the café. Then her body went limp against his, and he led her out of the door. The aroma of fear emanating from her made him harden in anticipation. He yearned to defile her beauty, to corrupt her innocence. Yet he also wanted her to remain resolute. She would be a toy that never broke so that he could abuse her anew year after year of her service.

Dae Lo craved revenge for the loss of status she had inflicted upon him when she ripped out his left eye. His teeth clenched just thinking of his superiors admonishing him for his carelessness in front of his subordinates. Every time he looked into their eyes now, he saw his humiliation reflected back at him. The *Gwanlyo* had sent a recording of his dressing down to everyone in the organization, and they could view it whenever they wished. Every time he met an employee, they could have just watched his humiliation. He never knew, and he became increasingly self-conscious. All of this because of a slender high school girl who had somehow managed to get the better of him.

Her very beauty and innocence had lulled him into lowering his guard that night. She had reminded him of a child, and it was only after she moved with an incredible speed to attack him that he realized the child possessed a deep power. This was why the *Gwanlyo* had appointed her to the Natural Police. They knew a butcher when they saw one.

He kept her body pressed against him as they walked down the street back to the building where Sey-Mi had been kept since she was hired. Her trembling sent shivers of anticipation through him. When they reached their destination, Sey-Mi moaned quietly and held back from entering the building.

“Still not cooperating?” Dae Lo deftly spun her around and clutched her throat in a viselike grip.

Sey-Mi choked on a scream as Dae Lo easily lifted her from her feet. He hooked his fingers around the waistband of her skirt and yanked it down around her kicking legs. Then he hurled her down the steps so that she crashed into the metal door below. Not giving her an opportunity to recover, he leapt down after her and landed on her knee. The bone broke with a satisfying crack, and Sey-Mi howled in pain.

Dae Lo grabbed the back of her head, spun her around, and slammed her face first into the wall. He ground her nose into the rough brick as he fetched the key and unlocked the door. Then he tossed her to the dirty basement floor and slammed the door shut behind him. Moving at his fastest speed, he retrieved the chains that Sey-Mi hadn't worn in days, shackled her wrists and ankles, and then tossed the key into the corner.

The bar once again forced Sey-Mi into a fetal position. She groaned, blood slipping down the scratches along her forehead and cheeks. Dae Lo crouched next to her. "This won't all be entertainment," he promised her. "There's a lesson you must learn, and you're going to get it tonight. We won't stop until you do."

Dae Lo cocked back his foot and kicked her in the groin, the tip of his shoe shoving past her red panties. Pleading for mercy, Sey-Mi writhed to escape him. Dae Lo shifted his foot and stomped down on her stomach, grinding her torso into the ground. He took his phone out of his pocket, sent a quick message to a subordinate, and said to Sey-Mi, "I have something special for you. This I'm sure you'll enjoy."

The excitement at her suffering felt explosive, but his voice sounded surprisingly calm. Dae Lo pointed the phone camera at her, turned it on and began to record. He was like a conductor. Depending on where he pressed his heel, on her groin, her stomach, her chest, the cry he wrung from her bore a different pitch. Her helplessness against him, half-naked and desperate to escape, flooded Dae Lo with desire. The urge to climb on top of her and take her as brutally as he could overtook him, but as he unzipped his pants, the metal door opened.

The smell of pizza wafted into the room, and his subordinate walked over and handed two pizza boxes to him. Dae Lo placed them on the floor beside Sey-Mi and flipped open the lid of one. "Sweet potato pizza. Your favorite, right?"

He lifted a slice from the rest of the pie, long tendrils of cheese stretching up along with it. "Smells delicious." He took a small bite from it. "Tastes awful. But what's to be done? The taste of rot touches everything except blood. It's one of the conditions that comes with employment in *Gwanlyo*." He took another small bite from the pizza. "But that doesn't matter, because we must operate in the human world. There will be times when we must eat, and there will be times when we must drink. Sometimes it will be a little food just to keep up pretenses. Sometimes we will have to stuff ourselves if the humans around us are also stuffing themselves. And do you know what we can't do?" He leaned closer to Sey-Mi. "We can't spit it up because it tastes like shit."

Dae Lo grabbed Sey-Mi, pried her mouth open, and shoved the slice in until her cheeks puffed up. He placed his greasy hand over her lips and growled, "Now chew, bitch, and swallow."

She choked on the slice. Dae Lo slipped his hand under her cashmere sweater and grabbed her nipple between the tips of his thumb and forefinger. "Get it down," he told her, "or I'll rip this off."

Sey-Mi tried. He felt her jaws working on the slice of pizza, desperation in her eyes as she struggled to get the bread, cheese and topping down. Saliva and vomit leaked between Dae Lo's fingers. When he removed his hand, food exploded from her to splatter the floor. Dae Lo shook his head. "Let's try this again."

He shoved another slice into her mouth, and clasped his hand over her lips until she vomited again. He tried a few more times, until the whole first pizza lay in an undigested mess on the floor.

Dae Lo squeezed her nipple, and with a sharp twist of his wrist, tore it off. Sey-Mi's howls filled the room. Dae Lo clenched his fingers around her other nipple and ripped that off, too. He dropped the dark flaps of bloody flesh into the vomited pizza, grabbed her by the back of her head, and smashed her face into the mixture.

"We will be here all night," he promised her. "And tomorrow night, and the next. You will not leave this room until you've consumed all of that on the floor. Do you understand?"

He lifted Sey-Mi's head, vomit and blood covering her face.

"Now eat." He watched with pleasure as she extended her tongue and slurped it up.

CHAPTER 17

Seoul blurred past Cheol Yu as he leapt from one rooftop to another. The starless sky stretched above him while the bright neon signs below illuminated the streets in a rainbow of garish colors. He managed to keep pace with Hyeri, whose shorter legs propelled her across the city at incredible speeds. She must have gorged herself on blood in order to move that fast. Would it matter in the end once they reached their destination?

Hyeri's foolish decision to alert the Natural Police to the location of his apartment would be the death of them both. Cheol Yu glanced over his shoulder and cursed. One member of the organization had closed the gap between them, and he didn't see the other. Where was he?

Cheol Yu slid to his knees across a graveled roof surface as the flat blade of a machete whistled above him. The second employee was right on top of him. Cheol Yu kicked up at the man, his heel connecting with the agent's jaw with a sickening crunch that flipped the man backwards. The other member of the Natural Police reached them and leapt at Cheol Yu, machete raised to strike. Cheol Yu rolled out of the way as the blade cleaved at him once, then again, barely missing him. The edge came upon him quickly, and Cheol Yu considered falling to the street below where humans walked.

Before he was forced to make a decision, Hyeri slammed into the attacking agent and knocked him back. She grabbed Cheol Yu's hand, flung him through the air to the next rooftop, and followed after him.

"We're almost there." Her hair flowed behind her like an ominous black flag. "I'll point out where they're keeping Sey-Mi. Go get her. I can take care of these guys."

"I'm not going to leave you to fight them alone!"

Hyeri winked. "Don't worry. I'm not going to hold back!"

Death lurked in Hyeri's insane gaze. Cheol Yu wasn't sure how many employees and humans she planned to shove into the grave this night.

"There." She pointed at a cluster of buildings past the Banghwa subway station. "You see that four story windowless building. They keep her downstairs in the basement. There may be one or two employees with her. If you're lucky, she may actually be alone."

Cheol Yu didn't think he would meet good fortune. He focused on building his speed and strength to optimize his physical prowess. Hyeri made a sharp right, snatched something from the bag, tossed the remaining contents to him, and shouted, "Go, now!"

She spun to the Natural Police directly behind them and threw a cloud of white powder with one hand, then doused him in brake fluid with the other. Smoke immediately erupted from him followed by a fireball that had him screaming and rolling on the rooftop. The second agent slid to a halt and maintained a safe distance from her.

Hyeri leapt to the next building and pulled back a dark blanket to reveal several large canisters. She spread white powder over the roof.

Cheol Yu jumped to the street below and checked to see what remained in the bag she had tossed him. Brake fluid and chlorine powder. Cheol Yu had never used either as a weapon, but it seemed like combining them created some type of chemical reaction. He reached the building that Hyeri had pointed to, glanced behind him, and gasped. Fires had sprouted on multiple buildings. The sounds of screaming humans followed by the piercing wails of sirens shattered the night. The flames had spread beyond the older buildings of the immediate area. A modern apartment building flickered, orange tongues sticking out of its middle floors. Humans stood on balconies, crying, calling for help. Fire closed in one, who jumped. And fell.

Cheol Yu shook his head, went to the door and grabbed the handle. He pulled it open and peered down the dark stairwell leading to the basement. Cautiously, he descended. A noise he found difficult to identify drifted up the staircase. It was a sound of slurping and choking, the sound of something hard slapping against flesh. Cheol Yu reached the bottom step to see a metal door standing slightly ajar. He peered through and quickly made sense of the scene displayed before him.

Sey-Mi was there. He hadn't seen her since that night weeks ago in his apartment when the Natural Police had ambushed him. They had definitely hired her, as only an employee could suffer what the two men were doing and still live.

A wide washbowl had been placed in front of her. An employee Cheol Yu had met before crouched in front of it. He remembered the man's name. Dae Lo, *one who punishes*. That was exactly what he was doing to Sey-Mi. He held her tightly by the hair. Cheol Yu saw bloody spots where he'd ripped her hair from the scalp. Suddenly, Dae Lo slammed her face into a washbowl filled with vomit.

"We brought this down just for you," he growled at her and nudged the bowl. "Now eat!" That was the slurping sound coming up the stairs. Dae Lo lifted her head again after several seconds. Cheol Yu watched Sey-Mi struggle to keep down what she'd consumed, the undigested food a mask over her face. She lost the battle, and hurled the contents back into the bucket.

Meanwhile, a second employee was positioned behind her. Sey-Mi wore nothing but tattered red panties. This man was thrusting a short, thick steel pole into her vagina with a force that rocked her body. Occasionally he used a second pole as a paddle, pounding the slick metal against her buttocks with incredible force.

Cheol Yu, staring at the torture, gazed into the face of his great-grandniece who bore a striking resemblance to his sister whom he had not seen since he was hired decades ago. A sharp, cold anger sliced through him. He poured the white powder into his left hand and took firm hold of the bottle of brake fluid in the other. He burst into the room hoping to surprise the two employees, but Dae Lo was on his feet in an instant and rushed him. Cheol Yu flung the powder at Dae Lo and squirted the brake fluid. As the powder puffed in a cloud around Dae Lo, the liquid splashed against him. White smoke sizzled against Dae Lo as his hands wrapped around Cheol Yu's throat in a crushing grip. The white smoke became flame, which engulfed Dae Lo as he lifted Cheol Yu off his feet and slammed him into the wall. Dae Lo screamed as the fire consumed him, but he didn't loosen his grip. Instead, he brought his body forward and spread the chemical fire to Cheol Yu.

The orange tongues buried themselves into Cheol Yu. The pain was instantaneous, and Cheol Yu cried out even as he smashed his fist against Dae Lo. The fire engulfed their clothes, danced along their skin and swirled in their hair. White smoke filled the basement.

It was as Cheol Yu had feared. Hyeri had sent him to his death.

CHAPTER 18

Everywhere Min Gun saw Hyeri land, a fire leapt up moments afterwards. Most of the buildings were *Gwanlyo* owned, but the wind blew the flames to one of the many apartment buildings in the crowded neighborhood blocks. Humans became trapped on balconies as flames quickly blazed up walls. Others attempted to run through the white smoke, but collapsed before making it out of the thick poisonous gas. In the distance, wails of sirens drowned out the screams of the dying.

Min Gun didn't know how Hyeri created the fires, but he knew she had the advantage. He didn't know how to counter this weapon she wielded with wild abandon. He assumed that she and Cheol Yu had come to this area for Sey-Mi, and raced to the building where they were keeping her.

He heard battle cries coming from the basement even before he reached the bottom. The fire raged here, too. Flames engulfed two employees while a third tried to avoid being caught up in the duo tearing each other apart. Min Gun saw this distraction had given Sey-Mi an opportunity. She had gotten the key and unlocked the chains around her wrists and ankles. She gripped the steel bar that had connected the chains and with an earsplitting cry, rushed forward at the third employee.

Min Gun could have stopped her. Time slowed, the moment stretching into eternity. Reality took on a fragmented, surreal quality. The disheveled Sey-Mi, clumps of her hair ripped from her head, dry blood stained down her thighs, tendrils of vomit clinging to her face. The third employee, dodging the orange tongues one moment, turned in surprise to Sey-Mi the next.

Min Gun could have disarmed Sey-Mi as she charged forward, the bar clutched in her hands like a spear, but he did nothing as she impaled the edge of the bar into the bottom of the employee's chin. She didn't stop at the impact, driving the man back until his head slammed into the stone wall. The metal bored through his mouth into his skull to erupt out of the top of his head in a splatter of blood.

That alone wouldn't kill a *Gwanlyo* employee. Min Gun doubted Sey-Mi had what it took to get the job done. He rushed into the room, grabbed her hand, and pulled her away as, with a roar, Cheol Yu drove Dae Lo into the third employee.

"Get her out of here," Cheol Yu yelled at Min Gun as the three employees whirled about in the flames consuming them. Min Gun pulled Sey-Mi out of the room, slammed the door shut, and locked it. He started up the stairs and came to an abrupt stop. Hyeri stood in front of him, a bottle of brake fluid in one hand, a bag of white powder in the other.

Min Gun didn't move; his eyes fastened on Hyeri's. Hyeri suddenly smiled so wide that it nearly spilt her face in half. This did nothing to dissolve the tension radiating between them.

"We'll play together again," she promised Min Gun, stepping aside. "Cheol Yu's final wish was to save his great-grandniece, and I owe him that much. I will set my last fire for the night." She started back up the stairs and said over her shoulder, "You better run."

Min Gun scooped Sey-Mi up into his arms and followed Hyeri out of the building. Hyeri scaled the wall to the rooftop. Moments later, a fire mushroomed up to lick the dark sky. The neighborhood burned bright orange, clouds of white smoke billowing up to fill the air with death. Min Gun ran through the twisting streets. He listened closely for the presence of humans as he neared the main avenue. The resounding wails of sirens permeated the air. Overhead, helicopters circled Banghwa. Most of the humans had been evacuated except for first responders in gas masks battling the fires around them.

Min Gun focused on the latent power within the remaining blood running through his veins. This act would drain him, but he had no choice. He pulled shadows around him, focused on his speed, and dashed out into the main street. Even in the subway, the poisonous gas had cleared the humans, but he kept up the speed and shadows to avoid being caught by the CCTV. He dropped into the subway tunnel and collapsed, exhausted, into a dark alcove. He looked at Sey-Mi, her eyes barely open.

"What happens now?" she asked weakly.

"Now?" Min Gun held her close as he considered the question. "Now, we come up with a convincing lie."

CHAPTER 19

Sey-Mi stood naked in front of the full-length mirror on the wall. Her body no longer bore scars from her last night with Dae Lo. Min Gun had given her healing blood potions over the last week, and her strength had returned to normal. She was finally able to enjoy the limited freedom the *Gwanlyo* had given her: a new apartment in Shinchon. Her own place where she could do what she wanted, within the boundaries of the organization's rules and regulations.

A strange feeling crept over Sey-Mi. She examined the emotion, questioned if it was wise that it existed. Yet she couldn't deny that it lurked inside of her: hope. She could begin planning on how to tear down the *Gwanlyo* so that she could see her family again.

She didn't know how large the organization was, and she didn't care. She would find a way to kill them all.

Sey-Mi checked the time on her watch and went into her bedroom to change. She had gone shopping at a nearby department store and had used up most of her monthly allowance on filling her closet with clothes. She pulled on a skirt, stockings, and sweater, and checked herself in the mirror. Her overall appearance had changed since she'd been hired. There was something different about the face that stared back at her. Something beautiful, even in her own eyes.

There was a knock on the door, and she went to open it. There stood Min Gun, his expression carefully blank. He had called to inform her that he and another employee were coming over. He had not told her how she should prepare, but Sey-Mi knew they both had to be careful. They had rehearsed their story multiple times in the subway tunnel before Min Gun finally allowed them to resurface at a *Gwanlyo* sanctioned business. They had gone through great lengths to devise the most convincing lie because of the man standing next to Min Gun now.

Sey-Mi bowed to them both. “Please, come in.”

The newcomer wore a pair of glasses with big, round frames and mirror lenses, a dark suit, and a blue tie. He carried a briefcase. He returned her bow before stepping into her apartment, Min Gun following after him. She led them to the table and invited them to sit down. The man opened his briefcase, took out a clipboard of papers, and laid it before him.

“The *Gwanlyo* has been put in a unique position,” he began. “In modern history, we have not dealt with such a precarious situation as this. Many of our properties were destroyed in Banghwa. Several of our agents were killed, as well as numerous mortals. As a result, the human government has started multiple investigations.”

The man looked at Min Gun, then Sey-Mi, then back to Min Gun. “I am the Advocate,” he said, “and I will need you to tell me exactly how our organization came to be in this unfortunate state of affairs.”

Min Gun and Sey-Mi exchanged brief glances, then began to weave their agreed upon story.

Thank you for reading! If you like the book, please leave a review on Amazon and Goodreads. Even if you don't like it, please still leave a review. Reviews help authors and publishers spread the word!

To keep up with more Nightmare Press news, join the Anubis Press Dynasty on Facebook.

Todd Sullivan teaches English as a Second Language, and English Literatur & Writing in Asia. He has had numerous short stories, novelettes, an novellas published across several countries, including Thailand, the U.K. Australia, the U.S., and Canada. He is a practitioner of the sword-fightin martial arts, kumdo/kendo, and has trained in fencing (foil), Muay Thai Capoeira, Wing Chun, and JKD. He graduated from Queens College with Master of Fine Arts in Creative Writing, and received a Bachelor of Arts i English from Georgia State University. He attended Bread Loaf Writers Conference and the National Book Foundation Summer Writing Camps Todd is currently working on a series of horror and fantasy novellas that tak place in South Korea. His fantasy novella, *Hollow Men*, is available for pre order at: https://www.amazon.com/Hollow-Men-Todd-Sullivan ebook/dp/B07YJ6X4QN/ref=sr_1_1?keywords=Hollow+men+Todd+Sulliva n&qid=1571404788&sr=8-1, and will be released December 2019. He ca be found on Facebook at: https://www.facebook.com/todd.sullivan.7 Instagram: denevius; or Twitter: @Denevius.

ALSO AVAILABLE
FROM
FRIGHTENING FLOYDS
PUBLICATIONS

MORE TERRIFYING TALES FROM NIGHTMARE PRESS

CHAINSAW SISTERS

When Sis wakes up in her father's backyard, staring at a rickety old shed, she can't remember iow she got there or even who she is. But she remembers Amy, the sister that disappeared ong ago, the same sister that she now hears calling to her from the shed.

When Sis enters the shed she discovers that Amy is only there in spirit, and she is speaking to ier through a new body, and that body just happens to be a chainsaw.

Amy reveals to Sis that she was murdered by a local crime ring and she needs Sis to seek evenge for her. Sis agrees to the task and as Amy guides her to the home of each man esponsible, Sis uses Amy's new body to hack them to pieces.

But the situation isn't as straightforward as it seems. As Sis comes face to face with each ian, she finds herself in the middle of unfamiliar flashbacks that put her at the scene of a einous crime of which she has no recollection. In time, she begins to believe that these are ot her memories and Amy isn't telling her everything she needs to know.

/hat lies ahead beyond the coming bloodbath is something darker and more disturbing than is could have imagined. Who is Amy? Who is Sis? And what connection do they both have the men she's about to murder?

nd why is her sister now a telepathic chainsaw?

ANIMAL UPRISING!

A lion, a hybrid, a bear – oh no! A goat, a gull, and a big black dog! Can’ forget the roaches, the deer flies, and the tarantula hawk, or the abominabl insect that rises from the earth! We got creepy crawlers and killer critters fo everyone. Oh, you want mythical creatures? How about a malevolent spiri posed as a fox, a rambunctious jackalope, or a herd of unicorn-gazelles on distant planet? Let’s not forget the supernatural silver stag with the power t raise the dead. Oh, did I mention the giant mantis shrimp? Yeah – we got giant mantis shrimp. Humankind really has their work cut out for them in thi collection of terrifying tales of beastly butchery. Need to know more? Chec out *Animal Uprising!* for all of the mayhem.

NIGHT OF THE POSSUMS

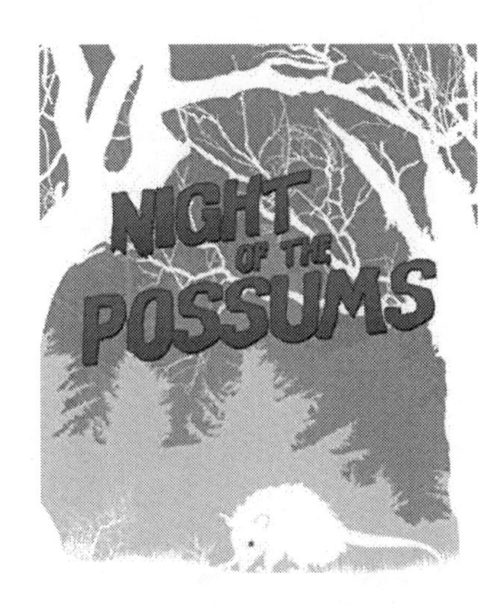

JACOB FLOYD

he night of the possums began on a chilly autumn morning around 2am in late October.

n a dark country road, a young man is torn to shreds by wild animals. The news of his grisly eath rocks the town. When a similar death occurs later that day, the town is in the grips of ear.

n rural Bardstown, Kentucky, opossums have risen up against the populace. People are being aimed and devoured throughout the city. These are not your ordinary opossums, either: they re smarter, stronger, faster, and far more vicious—some larger than any opossum anyone as ever seen, growing as long as four feet and as heavy as fifty pounds, with teeth capable of eaving bone.

s the flesh-eating scourge quickly spreads from one end of Bardstown to the other, a few of ose who survived the attacks band together in an attempt to eradicate the maniac arsupials. But, the number of the beasts grows by the hour and the force becomes too surmountable and the survivors soon realize escape is their only option.

ut, beyond the berserk behavior of the carnivorous creatures is a darker secret—something cient and unnatural that threatens all those who are bitten. Before anyone can find out what driving these opossums to kill, the survivors must battle their way through the merciless slaught of claws and teeth and leave the threat of Bardstown behind them.

IF YOU LIKE
THE PARANORMAL,
CHECK OUT
ANUBIS PRESS

HANDBOOK FOR THE DEAD

DON'T FORGET YOUR HANDBOOK…

Welcome all spirits! The Frightening Floyds present to you, *Handbook for the Dead* – a guide to help all new manifestations realize their functional perimeters.

Within this anthology, you'll read paranormal accounts from individuals who have experienced phantoms and disturbances that have not only chilled them, but also left them with some new insight into the supernatural. Now, they want to share their stories and wisdom with you. That way, if you're feeling a little flat, or even if you're a lost soul, you won't have to draw a door and knock.

Handbook for the Dead is sure to please the strange and unusual in everyone, and we promise it doesn't read like stereo instructions.

ALIENS OVER KENTUCKY

From the Frightening Floyds, the pair of paranormal enthusiasts who brought you *Be Our Ghost* and *Haunts of Hollywood Stars and Starlets* comes a new adventure int the realm of the unknown – *Aliens Over Kentucky*.

This collection includes the most noted extraterrestrial encounters from th Bluegrass State, such as the Kelly Creatures Incident of 1955, the Stanfor Abductions, the Dogfight above General Electric, and the tale of Capt. Thoma Mantell chasing a UFO through Kentucky skies. But that's not all. There are lesse known, but equally intriguing, reports herein, such as the train collision with th UFO, stories of unexplained crop circles and cattle mutilations, Spring-heeled Jacl the Meat Shower of 1876, and many eyewitness reports of various unidentifie crafts. You'll also read a couple of personal experiences from the authors, and eve Muhammad Ali gets involved in the alien action.

Join Jacob and Jenny Floyd as they dig into the mysterious cases and theori regarding Kentucky's "X-Files". Just be sure to keep one eye on the book and t other on the sky…

BE OUR GHOST

'he Frightening Floyds invite you to be our ghost as we take you on a tour of ıe happiest haunted place on Earth! In this book, you will read about much f the alleged paranormal activity as well as urban legends spanning the arious Disney theme parks around the world. From the haunted dolls of It's Small World to the real ghosts of the Haunted Mansion, there are many ɔirits here to greet you. And make sure to say "Good morning" to George at irates of the Caribbean.

njoy the spooky and fascinating tales in *Be Our Ghost*! And don't worry, ıere are no hitchhiking ghosts ahead…or are there?

PARANORMAL ENCOUNTERS

The Frightening Floyds present *Paranormal Encounters*: a collection of 1 tales of true ghostly experiences. From a malevolent spirit remaining in a apartment, to a loving phone call from a lost relative; from a house with sliding chair and slamming doors, to a snow globe moving across a bedroo from a possible past-life experience to a ghostly stranger in a radio statio this anthology contains several strange and unusual stories that are sure t entertain fans of the paranormal.

HAUNTS OF HOLLYWOOD STARS AND STARLETS

Explore the dark side of Tinseltown in this collection of paranormal stories, conspiracy theories, curses, and legends about some of Hollywood's most iconic names: Marilyn Monroe, Rudolph Valentino, Charlie Chaplin, James Dean, Jean Harlow, Clark and Carole, Lucille Ball, Michael Jackson, Bela Lugosi, Lon Cheney, John Belushi, and the King himself—Elvis Presley—and many more. Join the Frightening Floyds as they take you on a terrifying journey through the city of glamour and glitz!

Available on Amazon in paperback and Kindle!

BELLA

In an alternate 1800's America, where magic is real and dragons soar through the skies of the American frontier -

Topher had a good life, mostly. It wasn't great, but what can a young African girl expect living on the Edge of the World?

She had a shack that she shared with her Ma, she knew what vendors she could pocket an apple from, and was better than anyone with a spitshot. What more could a girl in the slums expect?

Then that chucklehead Wasco rolled out of the mountains like a toppled boulder. Topher had figured he might be good for a penny or two if she showed him around. Before she knew it he had her trompin' around the Blacklands, getting shot at, almost eaten and damn near gutted by some bull-headed dandy!

Jacob, who was about the handsomest gunfighter a body could imagine, might be some kind of monster. Old Ying turned out to be one of them wizards from the storybooks and Li had a magic sword!

All because someone went and took Bella and Wasco aimed to get her back, and Topher had been too stubborn not to follow him.

Yeah, it had been a good enough life. She just wasn't sure she was going to make it back to it, or if she even wanted to.

COMING SOON:

FROM NIGHTMARE PRESS:

Retro Horror
An anthology

The Gray Man of Smoke and Shadows
Todd Sullivan

Scratched
An anthology

FROM ANUBIS PRESS:

Haunted Surry to Suffolk: Spooky Locations Along Route 10 and 460
Pamela K. Kinney

Haunted Hotels of Virginia
Susan Schwartz

Kentucky's Strange and Unusual Haunts
The Frightening Floyds

FROM WILD WEST PRESS

The Dark Frontier
An anthology

Thank you for reading! If you like the book, please leave a review on Amazon and Goodreads. Even if you don't like it, please still leave a review. Reviews help indie authors and publishers spread the word!

To keep up with more Anubis Press news, join the Anubis Press Dynasty on Facebook.

Made in the USA
Columbia, SC
19 February 2025

54010736R00067